W9-CDN-091

Wanda Seasongood and the Almost Perfect Lie

Also by Susan Lurie

Wanda Seasongood and the Mostly True Secret

Wanda Seasongood and the Almost Perfect Lie

By Susan Lurie

Illustrated by Jenn Harney

LITTLE, BROWN AND COMPANY

New York Boston

Little, Brown and Company
Hachette Book Group
1290 Avenue of the Americas, New York, NY 10104
Visit us at LBYR.com

First Edition: August 2020

Little, Brown and Company is a division of Hachette Book Group, Inc. The Little, Brown name and logo are trademarks of Hachette Book Group, Inc.

The publisher is not responsible for websites (or their content) that are not owned by the publisher.

Book design by Tyler Nevins

Library of Congress Cataloging-in-Publication Data
Names: Lurie, Susan (Susan L.), author. | Harney, Jennifer, illustrator.
Title: Wanda Seasongood and the almost perfect lie / by Susan Lurie; illustrated by Jenn Harney.
Description: First edition. | Los Angeles: Disney/Hyperion, 2020. | Summary: Wanda Seasongood and the talking bluebird Voltaire undertake a mission to enter the Scary Wood and save Wanda's older sister Wren, who was kidnapped by the evil witch Raymunda.
Identifiers: LCCN 2019014148 | ISBN 9781368043229
Subjects: | CYAC: Sisters—Fiction. | Honesty—Fiction. | Memory—Fiction. | Witches—Fiction. | Magic—Fiction. | Bluebirds—Fiction. | Adventure and adventurers—Fiction.
Classification: LCC PZ7.1.L87 Wak 2020 | DDC [Fic]—dc23
LC record available at https://lccn.loc.gov/2019014148

ISBNs: 978-1-368-04322-9 (hardcover), 978-1-368-05689-2 (ebook)

Printed in the United States of America

LSC-H

10 9 8 7 6 5 4 3 2 1

For Ryan, Leila, and Jane

A Box of Air

It was two weeks after Wanda Seasongood's eleventh birthday, and she was about to set off on a frightening mission. She stood on her porch for a moment, enjoying the warmth of the morning sun. The air felt enchanted and dreamy. *Nothing bad can happen on a day like today,* she thought. Then something fell from the sky and hit her on the head.

Wanda stumbled backward but caught herself. She quickly gazed up to see a fly zigzag above her, then zip away. Just a fly.

How peculiar.

She waited for her head to stop throbbing, then picked up the object. It was a fist-sized rock with very sharp edges. Someone had written a message on it in bold letters: **See Attached**.

See Attached? Tied to the rock was a box. *How could anyone possibly miss this?* Wanda thought as she studied it. It was slender and wrapped with plain brown paper and the thinnest twine. She lifted it close to her ear and shook it, trying to guess what was hidden inside. The package was as light as a tissue and just as silent. *A box of air,* she imagined.

What a mystery this is.

How did it suddenly fall out of the sky?

Who sent it?

Wanda wondered if it might be a birthday present. Her parents had completely forgotten her birthday, which, at the time, had been fairly upsetting. But Wanda wasn't the sort to brood about such things. Still, she'd welcome a gift from them, no matter how late or strange its arrival.

Her eyes squinted behind her brown eyeglasses as she tried to read the small writing on the package. Her name appeared on one side, but the wrapping held no other clues.

She turned the box around and around, then gazed into the trees, searching for her best friend. He was a bluebird, and as odd as it might sound, she liked talking things over with him.

Now, before you judge Wanda as weird or eccentric, you should know that this was no ordinary bluebird. His name was Voltaire, and he could speak.

Long ago, in the 1700s, there lived a man named Voltaire, a well-known French writer. But the bluebird insisted that *he* was the real Voltaire, and since he could talk and quote the famous writer, it seemed somewhat petty to object to his claim. Besides, even though the bird was often befuddled, he was very wise . . . at least Wanda thought so.

I wonder where he is? Wanda sighed. He had told Wanda he'd be back in a minute, but that was half an hour ago. *I hope he hasn't forgotten about our mission.* Which she knew was entirely possible, since he was terribly absent-minded. But a fluttering through the trees quickly put her mind at ease.

"Ah! There you are!" she said as the bird landed on a nearby shrub.

"Sorry for the delay!" he apologized. "I returned just as soon as I remembered that I had forgotten where I was going."

"Well, you came back just in time!" Wanda said. "This

fell from the sky and hit me in the head." She held up the rock and the box.

"How exciting, Wanda! You've received a special delivery. Let's open it up and see what it is!"

Wanda studied the box and the pointy edges of the rock, now convinced that it wasn't from her parents. "I don't know . . ." Her voice trailed off. "What if it's dangerous?"

"Then *I* will open it, dear Wanda!" The bird flew from the bush and settled on her arm. He started to peck at the twine's knot to loosen it. "There's no time to waste. We will do this quickly so we can be on our way. We must . . ." The bird raised his head. "Please remind me: What is it that we must do?"

"We're going to save my sister, Wren, who has been kidnapped by Raymunda, an evil witch."

"Exactly! An unforgettable mission of the highest priority!" The bluebird inflated his chest to match the enormity of the task. "And frightening."

Wanda nodded. Frightening, indeed.

It was still hard for her to believe that witches were real. And that they lived in the woods so close to her home. And that she had actually fought one of them just weeks ago.

But it was true.

Wanda and Voltaire had ventured into the Scary Wood, searching for clues to uncover a family secret. Her parents had been acting strangely, especially when it came to Zane, her horrible, beastly eight-year-old brother, whom they seemed to prefer over her. She was determined to find out why.

In the forest, Wanda had made an amazing discovery—Zane wasn't her brother! He was Raymunda's son, and even more powerful than his mother, which Raymunda could not abide. So she'd turned him into a beast-boy, bewitched the Seasongoods to accept him as their own, and stolen Wanda's older sister in a trade.

To set things straight, Wanda had battled Raymunda and escaped with a potion that would break the spells and cure Zane and her parents. When the curse was lifted, Wanda discovered that Zane wasn't a child of eight, but a young man of eighteen, and she was very relieved to see him return to his home in the woods.

"Wanda, I now recall that I was supposed to tell you something about this mission," Voltaire said, shaking Wanda from her thoughts. "I do wish I could remember what it was."

Wanda wished he could remember what it was, too. Earlier that morning, he had mentioned it. He said it was something important that she should know *before* they left to rescue Wren. But at the moment his memory held no more than that.

"I'm sure it will come back to you." Wanda hid her disappointment with a gentle smile.

"Now, as for this package . . ." Voltaire began to peck at it again.

"Voltaire, wait." Wanda lifted her arm so she could speak eye to eye with the bird. "I don't think we should open it. Raymunda might have sent it, which means whatever's inside could possibly kill us."

"We cannot allow fear to rule our lives!" Voltaire stood firm. And before she could stop him, he pulled the string free with his beak. Then he ripped the paper from the package.

"Can this really be?" Wanda blinked hard as she held up the box. "Have you ever seen anything like this?" It was made of the thinnest, most delicate threads of silver and gold, braided and shimmering, and tightly woven to form a stiff, sturdy box. She searched for a lid or a latch, but there was none. "There's no way to open it."

"Let me try!" The bluebird pecked the top of the box—and his beak sank right through the strong mesh. When he lifted his head, the surface was solid again, with no sign that he had punctured it.

"It's magical! How marvelous!" he chirped. "Can you

believe it? My beak has suddenly acquired new powers!" His eyes crossed as he peered down at it with newfound respect.

"I don't think this has anything to do with your beak." Wanda pushed down on the top of the box, and as she expected, it moved under her touch. It was firm enough to hold its shape yet yielded to pressure—and this gave Wanda an excellent idea.

She pressed the top of the box again, harder this time—and her fingers sank inside. She wrapped them around an object and lifted it out.

It was a gleaming silver pen with the head of a horned goat at the top. It was beautiful and seemed practically weightless. Wanda thought that if she released her grip, the pen would float out of her hand. It was very unusual and a perfect gift for Wanda, who loved to read and to write in her journal.

She sat down and slipped her purple rucksack from her shoulders. "I have to try it." She took out her diary and started to print her name.

The pen didn't work.

She tried again.

Not a single letter appeared.

And this worried her. If the pen didn't write, what *did* it do? Surely, no one who meant well would send her an unusable pen. She stared into the silvery eyes of the goat—and they seemed to stare back at her. *Where did you come from?* she wondered. *Are you an innocent gift or not?*

Wanda had known that searching for Wren would

bring trouble. But she didn't expect it this soon, or that it would land on her doorstep.

And this gave her a reason to rethink their mission. "Voltaire, I've just decided to put off the search for Wren. We should come up with another way to save her."

She attempted to use the pen again, drawing inkless whorls and swirls. "My decision is final." She gazed up at Voltaire, who was perched on the windowsill.

"Wanda, I don't want to argue with you—but the pen seems to disagree." The bird nodded toward her diary.

There, on the paper where Wanda had drawn her invisible loops, letters had taken shape. She held her breath as they continued to form. The last letter was completed with a curl and a swish. Wanda gasped as she read the message:

Wren in Danger.
Leave at Once.

The Work of a Witch

"Let's go!" At the sight of the message, Wanda's doubts dissolved in an instant. She sprang to her feet, tossed the pen and diary into her rucksack, and leaped off the front steps. She was halfway down the path to the street when she heard her mother calling.

"Wanda! Where are you going?"

Her parents stood in the doorway in their dull red bathrobes. Her mother's hair, usually bouncy, was pressed flat to her head. Her father's eyes were still glazed with sleep.

"Oh, no. We have to turn back," Wanda told the bird. "I'll make it quick."

"Where are you going so early in the morning?" Her mother shuffled down the walk to meet her.

"Were you trying to sneak out?" her father asked, puzzled.

Wanda took a deep breath. "I'm going to find Wren."

"No! No! No!" Wanda's father dove down the steps and took Wanda by the shoulders. "We've already discussed this. Fighting a witch is just too dangerous. And you shouldn't go into the woods alone."

Truth be told, Wanda wished that someone else would go save her sister. And who could blame her? After all, would *you* want to fight a witch who wanted you dead? Not likely.

And besides, Wanda barely knew her sister. Wren had been stolen so long ago, Wanda couldn't recall a thing about her. But Wanda's parents were too frightened to battle Raymunda—so that left it up to Wanda. She remembered how proud and surprised her parents had been when she returned home from the Scary Wood the first time. It was just the encouragement she needed to face the witch now.

Wanda's mother tugged the ends of her belt, tightening her robe, then clasped her daughter's hand. "Please don't go. You and Wren are very different," she said.

"We worry about you making it out of those woods again . . ."

My mother loves me so much. Wanda's heart swelled with well-being.

". . . because you were never the smart one," Mrs. Seasongood went on. "You might not be as lucky this time."

Wanda's shoulders sagged and her knees buckled. Her heart was instantly crushed, her determination pummeled, and she was, quite frankly, too stunned to reply. She took a deep breath and instructed herself to focus on what was important—finding Wren.

"You're probably right," Wanda said when the shock had dulled and she could finally speak. "It's too dangerous." Then she headed to the garden at the back of her house.

The moment Wanda's parents lost sight of her, she vaulted over the backyard fence with Voltaire flying closely behind her. She ran through the leafy streets and up a deserted hill. She ran through a small town. She ran as fast as she could to flee from her mother's insult. She ran until she reached a meadow at the edge of the Scary Wood. Only then did she stop to catch her breath.

"My parents think I'm stupid, Voltaire. I never knew

they thought so little of me." Her mother's words had cut very deep.

"Don't be upset." The bluebird landed on her shoulder. "Your parents want to keep you safe. They simply lack tact."

"Wait. What are you saying?" Wanda's head whipped around sharply. Her frizzy reddish-brown hair whacked the bird and sent him hurling into the air.

"Tact, Wanda," Voltaire said, fluttering safely to the ground. "It's 'the knack of making a point without making an enemy'—to quote my good friend Sir Isaac Newton."

"No. No. Are *you* saying that I'm not smart?"

"I don't think I'm saying that at all. . . ." Voltaire brought the top of his wing to his chin. "Hmm . . . Is Wanda smart?" Head down, he paced the sidewalk,

contemplating the question. "Aha!" He stopped and lifted his head. "I would have to be smart to know the answer to that. Do you think *I'm* smart?"

"Yes, of course I do," she answered.

"Thank you, Wanda. Smart of you to say so. There! That settles that! Now, let's carry on." He rose from the ground and flew into the woods.

Wanda stepped from a field of bright, cheerful goldenrod into the forest's black shifting shadows, and a feeling of dread passed through her. Everything about these woods was disturbing—the musty smell that choked her breath, the darkness that snuffed out the morning light, the eerie, evil stillness. . . .

She thought about some of the creatures she had met the last time she was here. The Groods—horrible beasts who had tried to tear her apart limb from limb. The swamp creature, a gnome who had turned her to smoke. The nixie, a water spirit who had attempted to drown her. She shuddered.

"Nothing good happens in these woods," she murmured.

"Wanda, come quick!" Voltaire cried out.

She bolted through the trees and found the bird perched at the start of a path. "Are you all right?" she asked.

"Better than all right," he chirped. "Today is our lucky day! Someone has left a trail for us to follow. How kind."

It was true. Someone had placed a line of stones down the middle of one of the paths. It stretched deep into the forest, as far as she could see.

"We simply have to follow these to find Wren," Voltaire chirped. The bluebird took to the air, ready to leave.

It did look like someone was trying to help them, but a prickly thought began to claw at Wanda's mind.

Were the carefully placed stones really an act of kindness?

Would they lead to Wren—or straight into a trap?

When she studied them more closely, she saw that the rocks were similar to the one that had targeted her head.

No, this wasn't luck at all, Wanda decided. This was most certainly the work of a witch.

Take a Guess

"Voltaire, we can't take this path." Wanda frowned. "If the witch sent the message, these stones are a trick, and the trail will lead us directly to danger."

She gazed into the distance at all the other paths that now seemed to beckon her. "Our rescue mission is only one minute old, and we're already stumped." *What if my mother was right? Maybe I was just lucky last time.* She sighed. *Maybe I'm not smart enough for this task.* "Voltaire, we need to be Wren's heroes, and we're not off to a very good start."

"I must disagree! Someone else could have sent the

pen, and this trail *could* lead to your sister. Probably. Most likely. And that would be an excellent start!"

Wanda stared hard at the stones, as if glaring at them would make them give up their secret. "How do we decide what to do?"

"A simple question, easily answered," the bird chirped,

and Wanda's wrinkled brow relaxed. She knew she could always count on Voltaire for a sensible solution.

"We should guess," he said.

"Guess?" Wanda's brow tightened again. "But what if we guess wrong?"

"Then we'll guess again, and we'll be right!" the bird said.

Wanda didn't intend to insult him, but she let out a long, loud moan.

"My dear girl." He fluttered to the ground and began to lecture her. "There are occasions for groaning, but this is not one of them. Sometimes life leaves us no choice but to guess."

"But taking a guess is like giving up," Wanda said. "It's failing."

"Incorrect! A guess is never a sign of defeat. A guess is not an end—it's a beginning!" The bird stood tall and spread out his wings. "Wanda, 'no great discovery was ever made without a bold guess.' Another saying from my clever friend Newton."

Wanda knelt to study the stones, hoping they'd offer a clue.

"Trust in fate. Dare to think for yourself. Take action," the bird said. "Or simply put—we can't stand here all day. Take a guess, Wanda."

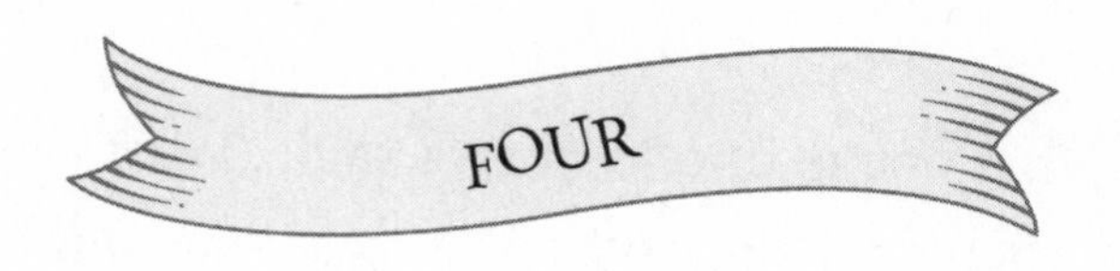

Between a Gurgle and a Snort

"We'll follow the stones," Wanda declared. And having made the decision, she suddenly felt taller and lighter, and she bounced into the woods to lead the way.

"Well done!" Voltaire fluttered behind her.

"I do think this is right!" she said, content with her choice. "I'm so happy you agree."

"Oh, but I don't," Voltaire said.

Wanda stopped abruptly, and the bird smacked into the back of her head. His wings faltered as he struggled to settle on a nearby bush.

"Then which path *should* we take?" Her voice cracked with uncertainty.

"Oh, this one is fine," Voltaire said. "I just meant to say that there's no right way or wrong way in the Scary Wood. They're all the same. They all lead to trouble. But at least there's nothing to fear at the moment!" He propelled from the limb and soared merrily ahead.

Wanda focused on the stones and ordered herself not to worry.

The woods were quiet. No chirping birds. No buzzing insects. No scurrying creatures rustling the leaves. It was an unusual silence, but the stillness also meant there were no lurking beasts, which helped Wanda stay brave.

Her heartbeat sprinted as she traveled deeper into the forest, farther from home. From time to time, she gazed ahead to keep the bluebird in sight. *If we need to escape in a hurry, we can just follow the stones back to the meadow. Returning will be easy,* she thought—and that's when she heard the whistling.

"Voltaire, listen," Wanda called to the bird. "It must be Wren!" She imagined her sister picking colorful wildflowers in a clearing while whistling the lovely tune.

Wanda and Voltaire raced through the trees, following the sound, anxious to reach Wren before they lost her. They moved quickly but quietly, gravely aware that Raymunda might be with her.

"Shh." Wanda stopped and put a finger to her lips. Her sister was just on the other side of a tall evergreen.

With Voltaire perched on top of her head, she slowly peeked around the tree—and her heart clenched for a beat. Voltaire's feathers stiffened.

This can't be, she thought. *This hideous creature can't be the one whistling such a sweet melody.*

He was wide and squat, a little taller than Wanda, with a head too large for his body. His light brown skin sagged under the weight of his wrinkles. He was hairy all over except for his scalp, where three lonely strands stood on end.

His bushy brown eyebrows shaded enormous ink-black eyes. His leathery ears were the size of Frisbees. They stuck way out and waved in the breeze. If a strong wind blew, his ears would catch the gust and lift him in flight, Wanda thought, if it weren't for the weight of his nose, which was broad and high and took up most of his face. His nostrils were huge, like two gaping, dark caves, and Wanda could stare right into them.

He stopped whistling to gulp some air, and she caught a glimpse of his teeth. There were a total of four—two on the top, two on the bottom—all black and rotting and crooked.

Wanda's gaze traveled from the top of his head down to his toes. He wore muddy green overalls and no shirt, socks, or shoes. He was an undersized man with oversized features, and Wanda had never seen anything like him.

"He's a troll," Voltaire whispered, and that explained all of it.

The troll trundled around the nearby trees. Between his sausagelike fingers he held a long, crooked spear that he kept stabbing over and over into the dirt.

"What do you think he's digging for?" Wanda asked Voltaire softly. But it was loud enough to alert the troll.

His head jerked up, and his hand went still. Then, between a gurgle and a snort, he grumbled, "Who's there?"

Wanda pressed her back against the tree. She closed her eyes and drew in a breath, waiting for the troll to move on.

Smack!

The spear whacked her hard on the shins. "OWWW!" she cried out in surprise.

"I knew I heard someone," the troll rumbled. He reeked of onions and garlic and mold, and Wanda held her breath to combat the stink.

"I hate noise, especially voices. These ears are so big, I hear too much." He pressed his beefy hands against them. "And I see too much." He blinked his large, bulging eyes. "And I smell too much."

"No argument there," Voltaire said, burying his beak in Wanda's hair.

Wanda stepped away from the tree. Directly behind the troll, she saw a wall of rock with a passage carved through it. "Look, Voltaire. The stones lead into that tunnel."

Voltaire pressed against her shoulder, nudging her toward the passage.

"It was, um, nice to meet you," she said, trying to make her way around the creature.

With a quick step to the side, the troll blocked her way. "Wait—" He interrupted himself with a sneeze—and a snot-covered snail flew out of one nostril. It hit Wanda's chest and bounced to the ground.

"Ugh!" said the troll, Wanda, and Voltaire in a chorus.

The creature groaned as he bent down to retrieve the snail. Then he stuffed it back up his nose.

"I wouldn't do that." Wanda nearly choked with disgust.

"I know you wouldn't. Do you think I'm stupid? That's why I stuffed it back up there myself," he snapped.

"Trolls are dim-witted," Voltaire whispered. "And overly sensitive about it. It's best we move on, Wanda dear."

Wanda tried to walk to the tunnel, but the troll met her, step for step, and wouldn't let her pass.

"Wanda, eh? I've heard all about you." He narrowed his eyes and gave a short snort.

"What do you know about me?" she asked, but the little man just shrugged.

"He hasn't heard a thing," Voltaire twittered. "He's just trying to scare you."

The troll stepped closer. "Are you ready for your test?" he snarled.

"What test?" Wanda backed away from his stench.

"That's my tunnel." He pointed behind him. "You have to pass a test in order to go through it. Are you ready?"

"I—I don't know."

"Well, you're off to a really good start," he muttered. "It's only one question. Pass it and go. Fail it and . . . well . . ." He rocked back and forth on his fat, dirty heels. "You don't want to fail it. . . . That's all I'm sayin'."

If trolls are dim-witted, the test should be easy, Wanda thought. Still, her mother's insult had curdled her confidence.

"Voltaire, I think we should follow the stones back the way we came and find a new path to Wren."

"I'm afraid that's not possible," the bird said, glancing behind them.

"Oh, no!" Wanda groaned. The stones were gone. "Where did they go?" She focused hard on the empty trail as if staring alone could bring them back. "Now what will we do?"

"Quit stalling. Are you taking my test or not?" the troll barked. "I wouldn't blame you if you gave up now. Word in the forest is your parents think you're an idiot."

"Wanda! He *does* know you!" Voltaire chirped.

The troll's remark riled Wanda with an anger that heated the air. She turned away from the path and watched him stab the ground with his spear. "Well, what'll it be? Are you stupid or not? Are you brave enough to find out?"

"I am *not* stupid." Wanda crossed her arms to show she meant business. "I'll take the test."

True or False?

"I love a quiz! Don't you love a quiz, Wanda?" Voltaire cheered. "Let's get started!"

"Move back." The troll poked his stick at Voltaire, who beat his wings in a fluster and settled onto a nearby bush. "You're not allowed to help."

"There's no need to be rude." Wanda stepped between the bird and the troll. "Don't threaten my friend."

"Calm down, Missy." The creature flicked out his tongue, which had hair on it, and Wanda cringed. "Now, let me think." He stroked his chin. "What will the question be?"

While he mulled it over, Wanda's mind was suddenly

and uncontrollably flooded with things she had learned over the years.

- JUPITER IS THE LARGEST PLANET.
- THE SQUARE ROOT OF SIXTY-FOUR IS EIGHT.
- PARIS IS THE CAPITAL OF FRANCE.
- WATER FREEZES AT THIRTY-TWO DEGREES FAHRENHEIT.
- IF AN ALLIGATOR ATTACKS YOU, JUMP ON ITS BACK.
- THOMAS JEFFERSON WAS THE THIRD PRESIDENT OF THE UNITED STATES.
- A TOUGH TOILET CLOG CAN BE CLEARED WITH A GOOD PLUNGER.
- BUTTERFLIES TASTE WITH THEIR FEET.
- NEVER WAKE UP A MUMMY.

Wanda's brain seemed to have a mind of its own, if that can be said, and the facts wouldn't stop coming. Afraid she'd forget everything she knew, she let them swarm until the troll interrupted.

"All right, here's your question!" He banged his spear on the ground—and chased every thought from Wanda's head.

"It's true or false," he said. "Okay. Pick one. True or false?"

"But what's the question?" she asked, wondering if she had missed something important.

"Don't be nosy. First the answer, then the question."

"That doesn't make sense," she protested.

"It's my test!" the troll hollered. "It doesn't have to make sense."

"Wanda, it's best not to argue." Voltaire flew to her ear and whispered. "Trolls have bad tempers."

"But I want a real test," she insisted.

"Let me see what I can do," said Voltaire. He turned to the troll. "Kind sir," he said politely, "could you come up with a different test? Perhaps one where the question arrives first?"

"I'll think about it." The troll scratched under his armpit. "Okay. I thought about it. How about some riddles?"

"I'm terrible at riddles."

"Then it's settled. We'll do riddles," he said.

Wanda tried to reason with the troll. "It's very important that I pass this test. My sister's life depends on it. And riddles are not a true measure of intelligence."

"Who cares? I like riddles," the troll replied. "Tell you what. I'll give you three tries. Three riddles, and we'll see if you can get one right."

And that was that. The troll would not change his mind.

"I'll start with an easy one," he said. "Here we go!" His

lips parted in a sinister grin. "*What two things can you never eat for breakfast?*"

Wanda gazed down at the ground to avoid his stare. And she thought. And thought. And thought.

The silence grew heavy. The air around her thickened with worry.

Voltaire ruffled his feathers nervously.

Finally, Wanda looked up. "I don't know," she admitted with a sigh.

The troll's eyes opened wide with glee. "*Lunch and dinner!*"

"That's not true!" Wanda argued. "I often eat lunch for breakfast."

"Lunch is lunch and dinner is dinner and neither is breakfast." The troll whacked his spear against a tree. "Now you've confused me. I'm not sure if you're right," he growled.

"Let's start over," Voltaire suggested. "That one won't count."

"Fine." The troll huffed. "Here's another. *What has every living person seen but will never see again?*"

As soon as Wanda heard the question, she knew she was doomed. Riddles turned her brain inside out—and this one did that and more. The harder she concentrated, the more her thoughts seemed to twist into knots. "I don't know," she was forced to reply again, and her heart began to pound. *I have two more chances.* She tried to calm her nerves.

"*What has every living person seen but will never see again?*" The troll took delight in repeating the question. "*Yesterday!*" he answered.

Wanda let out a frustrated groan.

"That was a hard one." Voltaire tried to make her feel better. "Don't fret. I'm sure you'll get the next one right."

"Ready, Missy? Here's number two: *What jumps higher than a mountain?*"

"Everything!" Voltaire shouted. "Mountains don't jump!"

"Disqualified! Disqualified!" The troll hopped up and down. "I said you weren't allowed to help!"

"Oh, so very sorry. I get terribly excited when I know the answer," Voltaire apologized. "Could we have a do-over for riddle number two?"

"NO!" the troll yelled. "You have to follow my rules!"

Voltaire was upset that he had squandered a riddle. His whole body slouched and his feathers rumpled. He flew from Wanda's shoulder and landed on a low branch to face her. "Do not despair!" he said, standing up straighter. "As the marvelous inventor Thomas Edison once said: 'Our greatest weakness lies in giving up. The most certain way to succeed is always to try just one more time.' And as luck would have it, Wanda dear, you have one more chance!"

With that, the bird's mood brightened. But Wanda was still a wreck. She was down to her last riddle—and her pulse raced faster than a high-speed train.

The troll stared hard at her with his big black eyes. "Here ya go. Number three. *What tastes better than it smells?* Think carefully, Wanda dear," he said, mimicking Voltaire. "This is your final riddle—and the last chance you have to save your sister's life."

Multiple Choice

What tastes better than it smells?

Wanda put her mind to the question—and a strange hush fell over the woods. It was as if all the creatures knew Wren's life was at stake and honored the moment in silence.

Wanda lowered her head, deep in concentration, and Voltaire perched stiffly nearby.

What tastes better than it smells?

She banished all stray thoughts from her mind. She didn't think about Wren or the witch or how much she hated riddles. She thought only about the question.

What tastes better than it smells?

"A *tongue*," she said softly. Then she raised her head.

"My answer is *a tongue.*" She spoke louder this time. "That's right, isn't it!"

The troll let out a long, stinky breath. "Congrats, Missy. You got it right."

"I got it right! I got it right!" Wanda shouted, so pleased, so proud.

"Hooray for Wanda!" Voltaire flapped his wings. "And now we can depart." The bird flew to the tunnel, and Wanda followed him.

"Not so fast." The troll blocked their way. "You're not going anywhere. You failed my test."

"What do you mean, I failed the test? I answered correctly," Wanda declared.

"Exactly," the troll said. "I always keep the smart ones here. Only the stupid ones use the tunnel."

"That's not fair!" Wanda cried. "You tricked us."

"Sir." Voltaire flew to Wanda's shoulder. "You can't be suggesting what I think you're suggesting." The bird was in shock—and not much surprised him. "Are you saying that to pass means to fail and to fail means to pass?"

"You two confuse me," said the troll. "I'm saying that she stays. Period. The end." He drew his lips together and let out a whistle. It was loud and shrill and nothing like the sweet tune Wanda and Voltaire had heard before. Then out of the bushes stepped two more trolls.

They were identical twins, dressed in identical overalls, blue and muddy, with identical rips in identical knees. They were younger than their friend, but just as bald and equally as smelly.

"I'll tell you what . . ." the troll said, glancing at his pals. "If you answer one more question, I'll let *you* decide what happens next. It's multiple choice. Pick A or B."

"I refuse," Wanda said. She was done with his antics.

"Refusing would be C, and there is no C. You have to pick one. A or B?" he said.

"Wanda, pick one . . . but stall," Voltaire whispered. "I need some time to devise our escape." He turned his head slowly to study their surroundings.

Wanda did not like to be tricked and would not, could

not, let the troll have his way. "I'll choose one—but you must tell me the choices." She clamped her lips closed.

"So stubborn." The troll shook his head. "Fine. Pick A, and you stay and play with us. Pick B, and we bury you alive." With the announcement of B, one of the twins produced a very large shovel from behind his back.

"Let me think. . . ." The answer was clear, but Wanda pretended to mull over the choices.

"Wanda! I've got it!" Voltaire's eyes gleamed with success. "Your worries are over." He turned to the trolls. "Wanda picks B. Bury her alive!"

Shovel

"Whaaaat?" Wanda cried out in alarm. "Voltaire, are you feeling okay?"

The three trolls stepped forward, eyes filled with joy.

"Don't listen to him! Please! He's somewhat befuddled." Wanda's hands shot up to stop them. "I'll stay and play with you."

"No! No! Bury her alive! Bury her alive!" the bird insisted.

"Well, what'll it be?" The troll swatted some gnats that seemed intrigued by his nostrils. "It's your life, Missy. You get to choose."

Wanda stared at her friend. Had his good sense abandoned him?

"Wanda." The bluebird settled close to her ear. "These fellows are trying to trick you again. You cannot play with them," he whispered.

"But surely playing is better than being buried alive."

"Never! Not troll games! They'll pump you with air, then try to fly you. Or inflate you some more and make you explode. They'll pull you like putty and try to stretch you. Then yank you so hard, you'll snap in two. You won't survive a single one of their games." The bird shook his head with great vigor.

"But if they bury you alive," he continued, "they'll need to dig a very deep hole." He gave a nod to the shovel. "And we will use that time wisely to slip away."

"You're taking too long," the troll grumbled. "We're going to jump rope." He turned to the twins. "You're the turners. She's the rope. Grab her."

"WAIT!" Wanda cried out. "I've changed my mind. Bury me alive!"

"That's our favorite!" The twins slapped their thighs.

The old troll led Wanda to a clearing in a circle of trees. "Here we are. The perfect spot for a burial." He handed Wanda the shovel. "Dig."

"Are you crazy? I'm not going to dig my own grave." Wanda tossed the shovel aside.

"Listen, Missy. We're in charge here," the old troll said. "And that means you follow our DO's and DON'T's. You DO what we say. You DON'T have a choice." He jabbed his spear at Wanda. "You dig. We bury you. Got it?" He headed off. "I'll be back when the real fun starts. Time for me to hunt for snails."

"He sticks them in his nose so the gnats can't fly up there," one of the twins explained. Then he pointed to the shovel. "Dig."

Wanda lifted the shovel with a heavy heart. If she had to dig, she and the bird couldn't possibly sneak away. "I'm sunk," she said as she stabbed the dirt with the shovel's blade. But then her face suddenly brightened. Help had arrived—in the form of a truly excellent idea.

I've Been Meaning to Tell You

Wanda shoveled and shoveled and shoveled. Her brow turned damp under the strain. The twins sat beneath the shade of a tree, first eating, then napping, then picking bugs out of their ears. But they stopped abruptly when the old troll returned.

"What's this?" he thundered as he stared into the hole. He had been gone for an hour, but Wanda's grave was only two inches deep.

"I'm losing my patience with you!" he bellowed with anger. "Dig some more, and make it snappy!"

Wanda started shoveling again.

"Stop! Stop! Stop!" The troll slammed his spear

against a rock. "Don't you know how to use a shovel? That's the wrong end! How stupid you are!"

"So true!" Voltaire agreed. "Just ask her mother. They don't come any dumber than our Wanda, which means, my good fellow, that we must be going. Because according to your rules, only the smart ones stay here."

And with that, Wanda dropped the shovel and left with the bird. Her heart thumped as they headed into the trees, anxious that the trolls would take up a chase. But the old troll just stood there, scratching his head. "Those two confuse me," they could hear him muttering. And by the time he had sorted out what had just happened, Wanda and the bird had passed through the tunnel and were miles away.

* * *

"A splendid plan, superbly accomplished," Voltaire chirped. "Good work, Wanda!"

Wanda thought so, too, and although her confidence hadn't mended completely, she was starting to feel much better about herself.

As they continued through the forest, they picked up the trail of the stones again, extremely relieved that these hadn't disappeared like the others. They made their way in comfortable silence until a question popped into Wanda's mind. "I wonder what my sister will be like. The witch kidnapped her when we were so young, I don't remember a thing about her. She's going to be a stranger to me." Wanda stopped so the bird could hop into her hand. "What if we don't get along?"

"It *is* possible that she could be dreadful. I've certainly known a few sisters like that. But lucky for you, there's always the other one."

"The other one?"

"Yes, Wanda. Of course, the other one. It seems you've forgotten."

"I don't think so," Wanda said, baffled.

"Oh, pardon. You're quite right. I'm the one who has forgotten. But how clever of me to remember it now." The bird cocked his head, delighted with himself. "Wanda, I've been meaning to tell you—you don't have one sister, you have two!"

Dark Magic

"*Two* sisters?"

This news came as a shock to Wanda, and she stopped abruptly to lean on a tree.

"Two sisters? How do you know this?"

"How do I know? How do I know?" The bird flew up high to a long, thin branch. Then he began to pace, taking bouncy bird strides as he considered the question.

"Aha! Suddenly it's become quite clear. When I was flying through the woods yesterday on my way to your house, I stopped to rest on a tree branch—and I heard someone say that you had two sisters. Yes, that's it!" The bird proudly puffed out his chest.

"Who said it?" Wanda asked. "Can you remember anything else?"

"Perhaps spending time with the trolls has twisted my memory—but I do believe I heard the word *twins,*" he replied.

"Twins! How could my parents have forgotten about twins?" Wanda shook her head. "The witch must have clouded their memories with her spell. She made them forget about a whole other daughter."

Wanda was deeply distressed, but the thud of footsteps put an end to her thoughts. "Voltaire, I don't think we're alone."

"Not to worry! I'll fly in the general direction of the sound and let you know who or what I discover."

"No, wait," Wanda said. "I'll go. If Raymunda is out there, she could cast a terrible spell on you, but she can't harm me."

Hidden in the deepest pocket of Wanda's rucksack was a locket that protected its keeper from any curse a witch could conjure. It was called the Enlightener, and it had originally belonged to Raymunda. The last time Wanda had roamed these woods, she found it in a cave where the witch had accidentally dropped it.

Wanda took it from her bag. The locket's lapis case

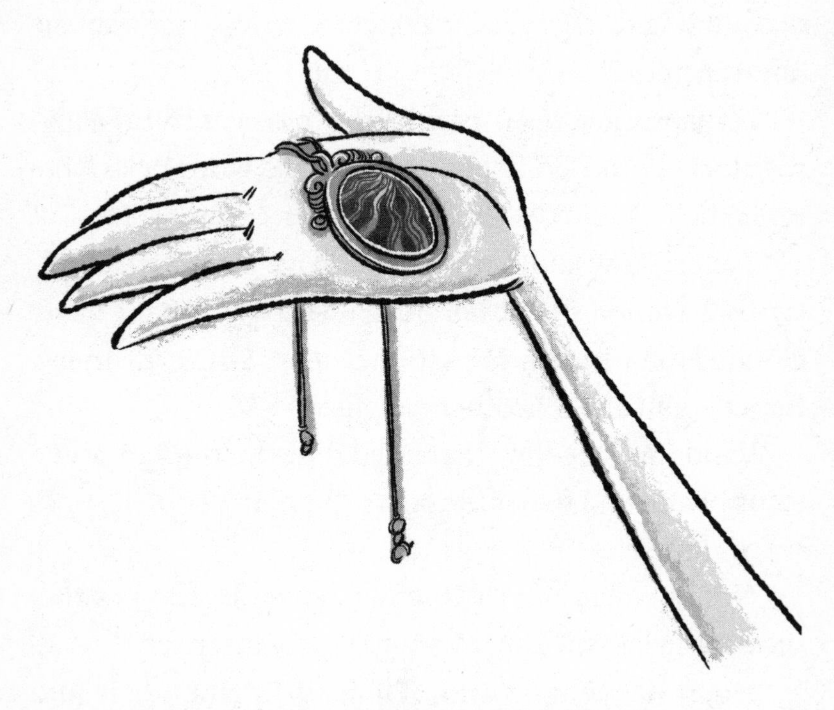

was the deepest blue, the shade of the sky at midnight. It had ripples of gold running through it. Like melted moonbeams, she thought, reassured by its presence.

"Hold on! What dark magic is this?" The bird's head jerked up and down in a bobbing frenzy.

"It's the locket, Voltaire. You've seen it before."

"Not that! This!" The bird glided to the ground and landed in front of the trail of stones, which had begun to glow. Wanda and the bluebird watched as they turned a deep orange, then a fiery red. They stood rigid as the stones quickly crumbled into embers.

We can still follow the ash, Wanda told herself, trying to stay calm, but a wild wind rose up and sent the cinders swirling through the trees. In seconds, every last trace of the stones had vanished.

"Voltaire, what's going on?"

"Clearly, someone doesn't want you to rescue your sister."

"How will we ever find her?" Wanda asked—and a deep voice answered.

"I know where Wren is."

A young man stepped out of the woods, and Wanda's hands flew to her bag, pressing the Enlightener close to her side. She knew this boy. His name was William and he was Zane's brother, Raymunda's younger son. He was someone to fear.

Liar! Liar!

"Hello, Wanda. How lucky I found you! It's so nice to see you again." Fifteen-year-old William was tall and very handsome. He had a chiseled face with high cheekbones and deep blue eyes. But it was his mesmerizing smile that dazzled Wanda.

He's a very bad person, she had to remind herself. *He's a witch, just like his mother and brother.*

"Well, it's not so nice to see you," she replied. "In case you've forgotten, the last time I was here, you brought me to your mother so she could destroy me. I thought you were my friend."

"Wanda, don't speak to this cad," Voltaire squawked. Then he glared at the boy. "Leave us at once."

"You're right to be angry with me," William admitted. "You might not believe this, but handing you over to my mother was the only way I could save you. I had to gain her trust first. I did, after all, help you escape."

"I suppose you have a point," Wanda said. "But how can we truly, truly believe you? You belong to the Coven of Lies. You told us that yourself."

Each witch belonged to a coven, William had explained to her. There were five covens in all—the covens of hatred, greed, jealousy, fear, and lies. A witch's power has to be fed, he had said, and in his case, every time someone (including himself) told a lie, he grew stronger. But he *had* helped her flee, and Wanda wondered if that alone made him trustworthy.

"Did you make our stones disappear?" she asked.

"What stones?"

"Aha!" Voltaire shouted. "That proves your dishonesty! You had to have seen them. You lie about everything—which means you know very well what stones she's talking about!"

"I don't lie about everything." William turned to Wanda. "Please, believe me. I don't know anything about stones."

Was he being truthful or not? Wanda still wasn't sure. "Voltaire thinks I have another sister here in the woods. What do you have to say about that?"

"I would have to say that I'm very surprised. I don't know of any other sister."

"Liar! Liar!" Voltaire squawked. "Young man, you are incapable of telling the truth. You twist everything to suit your own needs. You are evil. Wanda, banish this scoundrel from our presence at once."

Wanda understood the bird's mistrust. Why would anyone put their faith in a witch, especially one who had already betrayed them? But he seemed so sincere. . . .

"I'll trust you . . . for now," she said, which made Voltaire grumble.

"Well, I'm happy to see we're all friends again." William smiled, then brandished his wand and pointed it at Wanda. "You look cold," he said.

It was true—Wanda was shivering. A biting chill had fallen over the forest soon after William had appeared. With a snap of his wand, a cozy, flickering fire appeared in a pit in the ground. Wanda leaped back and gasped in surprise.

"Now, would you like something to eat?" he asked. And before she could answer, he burrowed through her rucksack and removed a brown paper bag that held her dinner—a simple cheese sandwich and a thermos of milk. "This won't do." He tapped the bag—and a three-course meal popped into view. There was

a steaming tureen of soup, a large ham, and mashed potatoes that rivaled the fluffiness of clouds. Freshly baked bread scented the air, along with the sweet smell of chocolate chip cookies—Wanda's favorite kind. Each appeared before her on a dish of fine china, along with fancy goblets filled with grape juice, all spread out on a wooden table he had conjured, too. With a final flick of his wrist, two fancy dining-room chairs popped into place.

"Very impressive." Wanda laughed, taking a seat. "I didn't know I was such a good cook."

Voltaire refused any and all of what the boy had to offer and pecked instead at some berries on a nearby bush.

"I can take you to Wren," William said when they'd finished their meal. "She and my mother live nearby. We'll go first thing in the morning, when my mother is out. She always spends sunrise in the deepest part of the darkest valley, at the stone meeting house, tending the witches' garden."

Wanda was eager to learn more about William's mother. Raymunda was an *Exemplary,* which meant she fed off the evil of all five covens. It was why she was so powerful. And why she ruled the other witches.

Raymunda feared nothing and no one—except Zane. Exemplaries were rare, but Zane was one, too.

Wanda had so many questions to ask William, but her head felt heavy and her eyelids began to droop.

"I don't know why I'm suddenly so tired." She let out a yawn. "I suppose it's because it's been a very long day and my belly is full." She wanted to tell William

about the trolls, and find out more about Wren, but she couldn't fend off her desire for sleep. "Let's catch up in the morning."

She left her seat and stretched out on the ground. With a wave of his wand, William made the grass beneath her as soft and plush as a comfy bed. "Mmm. Nice." She settled into it and yawned.

"Don't go to sleep, Wanda!" Voltaire whispered close to her ear. "This snake can't be trusted. We must stay up all night and keep watch. . . ."

"Yes . . . Voltaire . . . we . . ." she began, but her words drifted off. She had quickly dropped into a sound slumber.

* * *

The next morning, Wanda awoke with a start. The sky was still dark—not the black of night, but a deep shade of gray, the first sign of dawn. The sun would soon rise. She leaped up, very excited. With William's help, this was the day they would rescue Wren—

Except there was a problem, she saw right away.

Wanda spun in a circle and peered through the trees.

There was no sign of William anywhere.

Your Sister Is Quite Gruesome

"I'm not one to say 'I told you so,' Wanda dear, but in this instance I simply have no choice." Voltaire fluttered around Wanda as they set off. "I warned you not to fall asleep—and now that rascal is gone."

"You're right, Voltaire. I shouldn't have trusted him," she said, her gaze focused on the trail ahead of them. They had decided to search for the stones, hoping that somehow they would reappear, but Wanda's mind wasn't really devoted to the task. She was too busy reciting her list of wonders.

"I wonder if William made the stones vanish. I wonder if he knows what kind of danger Wren's in. I wonder if he ever tells the truth. I wonder why I thought I could trust him, even for one minute." Wanda shook her head, feeling altogether foolish.

"Everyone makes mistakes," the bluebird chirped. "No need to be so hard on yourself. Love truth, but pardon error, I always say."

The two walked on and on, with Voltaire hitching a ride atop Wanda's head, one of his favorite ways to travel. "We have two important things to do," Wanda began to think aloud. "We must find out more about my

other sister. First, though, we need to find Wren. But we have no idea where Raymunda lives."

"Aha! I am happy to report that we are not entirely in the dark on this matter," the bird said triumphantly. "It became clear to me just moments ago that Wren is in a castle. No, a cottage. No, a castle. How odd. I can't seem to decide. Let's say it's a castle. Yes, definitely a castle."

Voltaire's brain amazed her. Things came and went in no particular order, and it was always a mystery how a memory might just breeze in.

"Can you picture this castle?" she asked, trying to help him think a bit more clearly. "What does it look like?"

"It is huge, made of gray slabs of stone, with six towers and two turrets, and surrounded by a moat, but the drawbridge is down."

"How can you be sure the drawbridge is down?" Wanda asked.

"Because I'm looking right at it!"

Wanda stepped forward. Where the trees thinned out and between the trunks she could see it, too. "Voltaire, you're a genius!"

We're coming, Wren!

She and Voltaire moved out of the thicket and made their way to the drawbridge. *It's probably down because Raymunda is out, just as William had said she would be,* Wanda thought. It was just dawn, after all. She walked briskly, then broke into a run.

The front door was tucked into a deep, dark archway, and Wanda was relieved when they reached it—until she saw the size of it. It was wider than a truck and almost

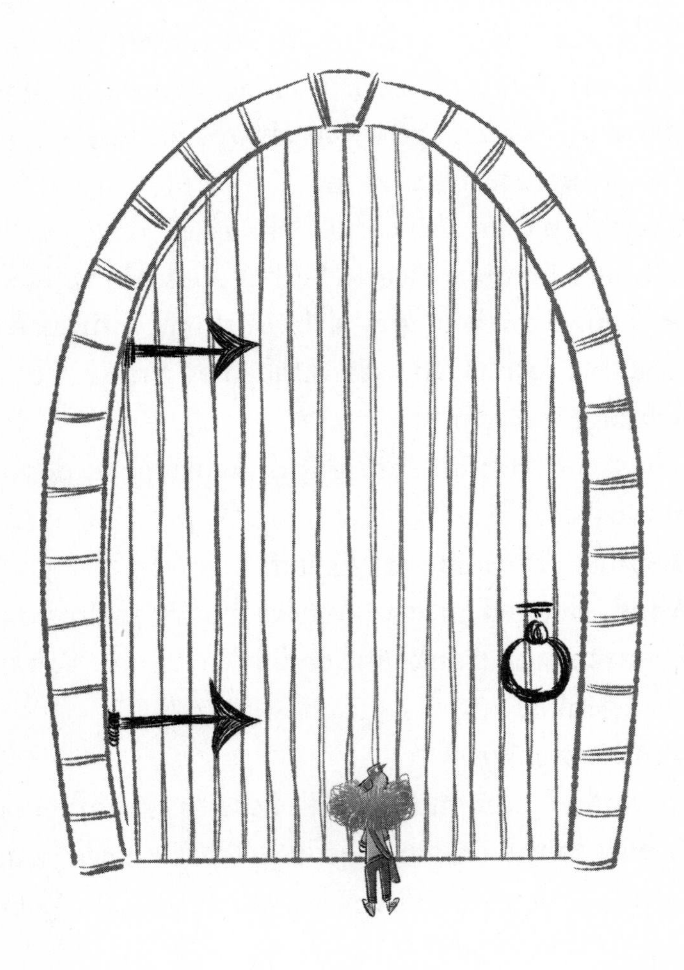

as tall as her two-story house, with an extremely large doorknob that was way over her head.

"I guess they don't use this entrance," Wanda whispered. "No one could possibly open this door."

"That's probably why they have this one." Voltaire flew to the side of the arch. Hidden in shadow was an average-sized door. Wanda turned the knob and it swung open easily. She took a deep breath and stepped inside.

A grand hall stretched in front of her. She tiptoed to the center of it and slowly turned to take it all in. It was the biggest room she'd ever seen. The ceiling was higher than the tallest tree in her garden. One wall was lined with enormous windows. The soft morning light streamed through their blue-tinted panes and cast a strange glow on her skin. The stone walls were covered with extra-large tapestries of flowery fields and flowing streams. Cut into the opposite wall were four open doorways that led to the other rooms in the castle.

"Have you ever seen anything like this?" Wanda asked, but Voltaire didn't answer. He had already headed to one of the doors and was fluttering in the opening to peek inside. In half a breath, he darted back to her, his eyes wide with alarm.

"What's wrong?" Wanda asked.

"I'm sorry to report that your sister is quite gruesome."

Wanda peered through the doorway—and gasped. A man at least twenty feet tall stood by a window. He had olive skin, shaggy red hair, and a long, wild beard. His thick red eyebrows hung over his very big eyes. Wanda drew in a sharp breath when she saw they were the shape and color of lemons. He wore a ragged brown shirt and too-short brown pants that his humungous muscles stretched at the seams. It was hard to imagine that any clothes could contain him.

"This isn't the witch's castle!" she whispered, too stunned to move. Her voice was low, but not low enough.

"Who's in my house?" With two mighty stomps, the giant thundered into the hall. "Ha! I know who it is!" he roared. "It's my breakfast!"

Flat People

Wanda had never seen a giant, and now her greatest wish was never to see one again. His arms and legs were as thick as tree trunks. His mouth was triple the size of a kitchen sink drain. A shiny gold ring pierced his nostrils. But it was the strand dangling around his neck that filled her with dread—a chain of people, strung together, eyes wide with terror, faces rigid with fear.

The sight of them shattered her daze.

"Let's get out of here!" she shouted.

Wanda raced through the grand hall with the giant stomping behind her. She yanked open the door they'd entered, but with the flick of his pinky, the giant

slammed it shut. He brought one of his huge eyeballs close to her face. "Nice!" he said, scooping her up and placing her in the palm of his hand.

"Put her down!" Voltaire shouted, but the giant ignored him as he started through the castle's rooms.

He walked through a parlor and passed a sofa as long as a bus. Wanda saw a dining room table that could seat a dozen giants or sixty people of average size. An extra-large library held extra-large books. And a glimpse inside a very big bathroom revealed a titanic toilet too frightening to ponder.

Wanda bounced in the giant's palm as he thumped from the front of the castle on the way to the back.

"Hold on!" Voltaire flew beside her. "I assure you, I am already planning our escape!"

"Voltaire, please look at the strand around his neck. Are the people hanging there dead or alive?"

Voltaire tried to get close to the giant's chest, but the creature blew him away with a leisurely breath.

The giant and Wanda entered the kitchen, a two-minute walk that would have taken Wanda twenty. "Here we are." He set her down on a large wooden table that stood nine feet off a blue-tiled floor. "What's your name, little girl?" He lifted her chin with a big, fat finger.

Wanda was terrified, but she thought it would be best

to hide her fear. "My name is Wanda Seasongood, and I demand that you deliver me to the front door. I will not stay here a moment longer." She shoved his finger away.

"Oh! I love food that fights back." The giant smiled and squinted to study her. "But I think you're too scrawny to eat."

Wanda's pulse slowed with relief.

"So I'll add you to my necklace instead," he said.

Wanda could see the strand of people clearly now. They hung hand-in-hand, reminding her of a paper-doll chain. They were, without a doubt, very dead. Her heart began to pound faster again.

"Leave her alone!" Voltaire had found his way to the kitchen and landed on the table right beside her.

"Did someone speak?" The giant leaned over and placed his face at the table's rim to get a better look at the talking speck. "Ahhhh. You're a bird, not a crumb." His bushy red beard shook with laughter. "I think I'll add you to my collection, too." With one of his fingers, he lifted the strand of people around his neck. "It could use something feathery in your shade of blue. But I'll start with the girl."

"You'll do no such thing," Voltaire squawked at the giant. "You can't hold her here, and I will not allow you to wear her. Haven't you heard of human rights?"

The bird hopped to the edge of the table and stared into one of the giant's lemon-colored eyes. "You must treat all people with dignity, fairness, equality, and respect. And they must never, ever, be made into jewelry. So, if you would kindly help Wanda down, we'll show ourselves out."

"Of course I've heard of human rights. I'm human, too," the giant replied. "I'm just a bigger human, which means I have more rights."

"Sir, it doesn't work that way." Voltaire flapped his wings.

"It does in this castle," the giant growled at Voltaire. "I've changed my mind. I think I'll start with you first."

The giant slipped the chain over his head, reached for Voltaire—and the bird took off. "Oh, well. Looks like you've just moved to the front of the line." The monster grinned at Wanda. "Ready?"

Dead Man's Chest

"Fear not, Wanda! I will employ my brains to save you!" cried Voltaire.

The bird circled the kitchen to gather speed. Then he launched headfirst into the giant's hand, and the necklace flew from the monster's fingers.

"That wasn't very nice," the giant grumbled. He quickly leaned over to catch the tumbling strand before it fell to the floor. "Bird, you leave me no choice. I will stuff you into my ear tonight and use you as a swab to dislodge the wax." He caught the necklace, but as he straightened up he smacked his head hard on the kitchen table. So hard, in fact, he knocked himself out.

He crashed to the floor with a wall-trembling thud.

Wanda leaped from his fingers and ran.

She and Voltaire charged down one hallway into another through chambers they hadn't seen before. But they seemed to be getting nowhere fast.

"Are we running in circles? I do hope we're not chasing ourselves." Voltaire's little body heaved with exhaustion.

"In here!" Wanda ducked into a room so they could catch their breath.

"What *is* all this?" she said, still gasping for air.

Scattered on a wooden table were human skulls, shrunken heads, feathers, fish bones, and braids of hair. The sun streamed in through a high, dusty window, lighting everything in a gauzy glow.

She moved to a wall where green glass bottles were lined up on a shelf. They were the old-fashioned kind, with cork stoppers instead of lids, and a metal sign beside them read: TONICS FOR CURSES AND REMEDIES FOR WHAT AILS YOU.

Wanda had never seen such an assortment of oddities, some charming, some ghastly. Antique dolls next to squirrel-jaw necklaces. Vintage mirrors beside mummified bats. Colorful crystals next to shiny, dead beetles.

DEAD MAN'S CHEST

On a shelf in a corner, a small, weathered trunk caught her eye. She brushed off the dust to read the letters carved into the lid: DEAD MAN'S CHEST.

"Wanda, we really should be going." Voltaire's breathing had slowed. "Before that vulgar fellow wakes up."

Wanda knew they should leave. But the chest intrigued her. She had to take a quick peek. She opened it and read the words inside the lid: FOR LIFE'S UNCERTAINTIES. TO BE USED FOR EVERYDAY PREDICAMENTS AND EXTRAORDINARY CIRCUMSTANCES.

She gasped at the hideous objects inside. There was a rotted tooth in a cardboard box, labeled: FOR SUFFERERS. She had read an old wives' tale that claimed a dead man's tooth could cure the pain of a toothache. Dead Man's Magic. Wanda had thought it was just a superstition. Now, staring into the chest, she wasn't so sure.

In another box, she saw a thumb that said: FOR WANDERERS. There was an eyeball: FOR SEARCHERS. And a pair of what she thought might be dried-out lips: FOR TRUTH SEEKERS. There was more, but Wanda stopped reading when she heard the giant groan.

"He's up!" Voltaire squawked. "Let's go!"

Wanda wasn't a thief. She would never ever dream of taking something that didn't belong to her. But what if those lips could reveal William's lies? And the eyeball could see where Wren was? *They could be so helpful,* she thought, *and I'll simply be borrowing them. . . .*

"Wanda, we must be off!" Voltaire warned her. His gaze remained steady as he stared down the hall.

She reached into the chest . . . but hesitated. The thought of touching a dead man's eyeball and dried-up lips made her stomach flip.

"Wanda, I hear footsteps. He's on the move."

Still . . . she couldn't resist.

She reached into the box—and the lid slammed down on her wrist. "OW!" She felt around for the lips and eyeball, grabbed them, and yanked her hand free.

"Okay! Let's go!" She and Voltaire fled from the room and ran into another—but stopped when they saw it had three ways out. "Which door should we take?" she cried. And that's when she felt a wiggle in the palm of her hand.

She opened her fist—and was more than surprised.

She hadn't taken the lips or the eyeball.

She was holding the thumb—and the moment she looked at it, it started to spin.

You'll Be Back

Voltaire, come quick!" Wanda stared at the dead man's thumb as it whirled faster and faster and began to grow hot.

"Gadzooks, Wanda!" The bird's feathers stood up in alarm. "We must find a cure for that!"

"It's not my finger," Wanda explained—and the thumb came to a jittery stop. After a little shimmy and a final shake, it stiffened—and pointed to the door on the right. "I think it's trying to help us!"

"I think so, too!" Voltaire shot through the doorway with Wanda behind him. They flew down to a cellar that reeked of dead things and rot.

The thumb twitched again, then pointed left. "This

way!" Wanda shouted, allowing the thumb to guide their flight.

It led them upstairs and downstairs in zigzags and circles. Through rooms long abandoned, where Wanda's footprints left marks in the dust.

"Where is it taking us?" Wanda worried as the giant's footsteps grew heavier. And louder. And frighteningly close.

They ran and ran in search of an exit. The floor now shook from the monster's lumbering gait. "You can't escape me!" his gruff voice thundered, making Wanda's heart pound as loudly as her feet.

They followed the thumb wherever it pointed, but Wanda's legs began to feel weary and weak. Then, just as her knees started to buckle, the grand hall they'd first entered came into view!

They rushed outside and dashed over the drawbridge. They ran at top speed and didn't let up.

When they reached the edge of the forest, they heard a loud cry behind them. "I'm saving a spot for you, Wanda Seasongood." The giant stood in the doorway, holding the necklace high. "You'll be back sooner or later. I've seen it in the dead man's eye."

What Is That Horrible Wailing?

What an excellent escape! I am a bird who has conquered a giant with my small but superior head. But I am also humble, so I must thank the thumb for its excellent guidance . . . and then we must return it."

"Return it?"

Crashing into the giant must have rattled his brain, Wanda thought. "I really don't think we should go back there," she said, hoping the bird wasn't permanently crazy.

"But the thumb doesn't belong to us," he replied. "Wanda, we are not thieves."

"No, we're not," Wanda agreed. "But the thumb might help us find Wren."

"True enough," he replied. "But, I repeat, that ghastly digit isn't ours. No, Wanda, we will have to rely on our own wits to rescue your sister." It was clear Voltaire would not change his mind.

"Fine," Wanda said, giving in. "We'll bring it back. I'll drop it at the giant's door, then run."

"Perfect." The bird reversed direction and started back to the castle, but Wanda remained where she was. "Why are you dawdling?" he asked.

"I'm not dawdling. My feet won't budge. Watch." She struggled to lift them, but they stayed stuck to the spot.

"Perhaps it's your shoes." Voltaire gave them a thoughtful glance. "Something might be bogging them down."

Wanda attempted to slip them off. But the tips clamped down her toes, and the harder she yanked, the tighter they held. She tried to sit and think about the problem, but the most she could manage was an uncomfortable squat.

"There is something powerful in the woods that wants to keep me here," she said, nervously peering between the trees.

"Indeed, there is—and it's in your rucksack!" the bird announced, staring at the outer pocket, which had begun to pulse.

"Oh, that," Wanda said, slipping off her bag to take the thing out.

It was the dead man's thumb. She set it in her palm, and it began to fling wildly about.

"What's wrong with it?" she asked.

"I might be mistaken," Voltaire said, "but I think it's upset." The thumb gave one last convulsion and then aimed in the direction that would take them *away* from the castle.

"Hmm." Wanda tried to walk where it pointed, and her feet moved with ease. "I guess we can only walk where it wants us to go. Do you think it's trying to keep us safe from the giant?"

"Oh, I doubt that," the bird chirped. "More likely it's angry and taking us someplace unpleasant. This is probably the dead man's revenge because we stole his thumb. Which makes me wonder . . ." Voltaire scratched his head with the tip of his wing. "What do you suppose he did to the fellow who chopped it off?"

* * *

Hours later, Wanda and the bird were still wandering the forest, with the dead man's thumb leading the way. Springtime had somehow missed this part of the Scary Wood. The tree trunks here were thin and bent. Not a single leaf hung on the warped branches. The ground was gray and parched. When Wanda's shoes kicked up the dirt, it coated her throat and made her choke. Everything here was still winter bare, and an aura of death hung in the air.

And then a screech rang out through the woods. It was loud and shrill and held more pain than a human could suffer. It bounced off the bone-dry trees and filled Wanda's head with its agony.

"What is that horrible wailing?" Wanda wanted to clutch her ears to shut it out, but she was afraid to put the dead man's thumb back in the pocket of her rucksack.

"Not to worry. That's just Brona," Voltaire said. "She's a shrieker, all right."

"Why is she howling like that? Is she hurt?"

"Oh, no. She's perfectly fine." Voltaire fluttered to Wanda's shoulder. "She's a banshee. She only screams that way when someone's about to die."

The Banshee

"Someone . . . someone like who? One of us?" Wanda's eyes widened at the thought.

"Most definitely," the bird chirped. "She's the banshee of the Scary Wood, so it's always someone in the forest—and usually someone close by."

The banshee's screams grew louder.

"I don't want to meet her." Wanda stared at the dead man's thumb, settled in the palm of her hand.

"Wanda, dear, we don't really have a say in the matter. The thumb seems to be in charge."

The banshee let out another howl. This one was so laden with misery and grief, it pierced Wanda's heart. Then a biting breeze rushed through the trees.

"She's here." Wanda watched the creature float in on the wind, her feet hovering inches above the ground. When she reached them, she dropped down with a loud *plop*.

"She's not at all what I thought the messenger of death would look like," Wanda whispered to the bird, who had perched on a bush beside her.

Wanda had expected an old withered woman, ghostly pale with rotted black teeth. But Brona was so much the opposite. She was younger than Wanda's mother, plump and hearty. She had creamy skin and a mountain of dark magenta hair in springy curls. Her cheeks held a rosy glow, and she smelled like lilies, which made Wanda sneeze.

"Hello, Sweetie." The banshee handed Wanda a tissue. "You don't look horrified to see me. That's good. That means I'm not here for you. Maybe. Mind if I sit? All that howling can drain a spirit."

The banshee had on a sleeveless, flowery shift, something Wanda's grandmother might wear, and she tucked it between her legs as she plunked herself onto a large rock.

"Ahhh, that's better." She wiggled her bare toes. "So, if I'm not here to announce your death, what *am* I here for?"

She stared at Wanda with her dark amber eyes.

"Wait a minute. You wouldn't happen to have an extra thumb on you?"

"Yes, I do!" Wanda held up the dead man's thumb for Brona to see.

"Bingo!" The banshee snapped her fingers. "I'll take that, Pumpkin." She waved her hand, beckoning Wanda to give it to her.

Wanda placed the dead man's thumb in Brona's palm, happy to be rid of it at last.

"You might not be able to hold on to it," Voltaire warned her. "It's grown quite attached to Wanda."

"Not a problem, Snookums. You'll see," Brona said to the bird, then turned to Wanda. "This thumb is your ticket to the Doors of Destiny. When the dead man's thumb leads you to me, I lead you to the Doors."

"What are the Doors of—" Wanda started, but Brona put up her hand to stop her.

"First things first," she said. She held out the dead man's thumb, took a deep breath, and exhaled a mighty blast of air. Her breath was so strong, it made Wanda's skin flap against her bones and sent Voltaire spiraling through the trees. The thumb went soaring out of sight.

“One of my special talents.” She brushed her hands together at a job well done. “I always know exactly where things need to go.”

Voltaire fluttered down from the branches and stopped in front of Brona. “This is superb,” he told her.

"How lucky you're here! Please send me where I need to go to remember a lie that I heard about Wanda."

"It doesn't work that way, Fluffy." Brona gave him a sideways glance.

"A lie?" Wanda asked Voltaire. "You never mentioned a lie."

"I know! Isn't it thrilling? It's amazing what you can almost remember if you put your mind to it." The bird turned to Brona. "Let's give it a try. You might want to take a *very* deep breath, in case I have to travel far." He looked over his shoulder at Wanda. "I shall return straightaway with important news, I hope!"

A lie.

A lie about me.

What could it be? Wanda wondered.

"All right, then! Let's get on with it!" Voltaire positioned himself directly in front of the banshee. He closed his eyes to shield them from her powerful breath.

"Sorry, Cutie," Brona said to the bird. "No can do. Really. I send only dead things away."

"Voltaire, can you remember anything about this lie?" Wanda asked.

"Yes, yes. Let's see. There must be something." The bird began to pace the dry earth, his little feet kicking up small puffs of dust. "Aha!" He stopped. "There *is* more I remember!" he said, quite pleased.

"What is it?" Wanda's curiosity rose to a peak.

"This lie is the key to every strange thing that has happened to you and will happen still."

Upon hearing this, Wanda's breath faltered and her world started to spin. This was a powerful lie, both grand and grave. What could it possibly be?

"Is there anything else you can recall? Think," Wanda implored. "Please, think!"

As much as he tried—and he tried very hard—this was as far as the bird's memory could stretch. "Fear not, Wanda," he chirped. "I'm certain the details of this lie are on their way! My memory hasn't failed me yet!"

"I'm sorry, Brona. I can't go to the Doors of Destiny, whatever they are. I must keep searching for my sister and help Voltaire uncover this lie."

"Wish you had a choice, Honeybunch. But you don't. You give me the thumb; I take you to the Doors of Destiny. It's in the handbook, believe me. Actually, you don't have to believe me. Ask your feet. They'll only follow me now," the banshee said.

Brona put her hands on her thighs, leaned over, and with a groan, stood up. "Ready?"

"No. I'm not ready. I don't want to go," Wanda objected, "and I certainly won't move until you tell me: What are the Doors of Destiny?"

"Sugar, trust me." Brona floated up from the ground. "You don't want to know."

The Doors of Destiny

It was true. Wanda could only follow Brona. She shuffled along, trying with every other step to outsmart her own feet. She'd meander off the path as if by accident, but her shoes would tighten around her heels and toes and always set her straight.

The three headed off through the woods for the Doors of Destiny. Voltaire sat on Wanda's shoulder, and Brona floated ahead of them, slightly off the ground.

Wanda was relieved to leave this part of the bleak and lifeless forest. Which isn't to say that she felt any calmer. Because she didn't. Her thoughts turned from the lie to the Doors of Destiny. "Voltaire, have you ever heard of these doors?"

"Never!" the bird chirped. "But they do sound intriguing!"

Wanda thought they sounded more frightening than intriguing, so she moved on to the next worry that consumed her. "We've been in the Scary Wood for two days, and the only thing we've managed to do is fail to find my sister." Her mouth turned down in a deep frown and her shoulders drooped.

"No, no, no, Wanda! We have not failed. As Thomas Edison said, we've 'just found ten thousand ways that won't work.' Wanda, dear, we are just like Thomas—on the brink of a great discovery!"

Wanda wished she could be as hopeful as Voltaire. She tried to think positive thoughts, but on this forced march, it was difficult to imagine that anything would be fine.

"How much farther is it?" Wanda asked the banshee after they had walked quite a distance.

"We're getting closer," Brona said, landing lightly on the ground to walk the rest of the way.

"Are the Doors of Destiny real doors?" Wanda thought if she could learn more about them, she'd feel less nervous.

"Yes, they're real doors," Brona replied without glancing back.

"In a house?"

"No, not in a house exactly."

"Then where?"

"Be patient, Gumdrop. Besides, you're better off not knowing more until we get there."

"Well, knowing *something* will be better than knowing nothing. At least that way I'll be able to prepare myself."

"Doubt it, Doll. Haven't seen that happen yet. But fine, if you think it will make you feel better. . . ." Brona waited for Wanda to catch up before she continued.

"Behind the Doors of Destiny, you'll find either your destiny or your death. Happy now?" Brona touched Wanda's shoulder, and in that instant, Wanda could see the banshee as she truly was.

Her face was gaunt and pulsed with knotty blue veins. Her lips were sunken and cracked. Her eyes were two solid black orbs. The skin on her body hung off her bones—and Wanda could see right through her.

The image flashed by so quickly, for a moment Wanda thought she hadn't seen it at all. She shuddered at the sight and continued to walk in silence, concentrating on slowing her racing heart.

"Well, here we are," Brona announced.

"We are?" Wanda said, confused.

Tucked in between two large trees stood two little gray buildings that looked like small closets. On one door, Wanda could see the number one. On the other, the number two.

"Those look like Porta Potties," Wanda said, scratching her head. "The Doors of Destiny are outdoor toilets?"

"Now that you mention it, they do look like those, don't they?" Brona grunted as she lowered herself onto a log so she could sit. "Trust me, they're not. Go read the sign on the tree, Cupcake, while I rest my tootsies."

Wanda walked up to the tree on the left where she saw a long wooden sign hammered into the trunk. Voltaire landed on her shoulder as Wanda read:

Choose Your Destiny
Some people use doors to keep things out.
Some people use doors to let things in.
Which are you?
If you are a person who thinks it's wiser to stay safe, select Door #1.
If you are a person who likes to explore possibilities, select Door #2.

"So, which will it be, Cookie? Door number one, or door number two?"

1
2
Choose Your Destiny
Some people use doors
to keep things out.
Some people use doors
to let things in.
Which are you?
If you are a person who
thinks it's wiser to stay
safe, select Door #1.
If you are a person who
likes to explore possibilities,
select Door #2.

"I—I don't know," Wanda said. "Don't rush me."

"That's what they all say." Brona blew out a breath that sent her magenta curls bouncing. "My advice: Don't overthink it. Go with your gut."

"Voltaire." Wanda looked at the bird. "What kind of person do you think I am?"

"No, no." Brona waved her hand. "Don't ask the bird. This is one you have to decide for yourself."

"Keep things out. Let things in. Keep things out. Let things in." Wanda paced in front of the doors, occasionally gazing at them to see if they offered any hints.

Finally, she stopped in front of Brona. "I'm ready," she said. "I am definitely a person who lets things in. I choose door number two."

"Reeeeally?" Brona said. "Well, that's in-ter-est-ing."

"What's *that* supposed to mean?" Wanda felt shaky enough—she didn't appreciate the banshee casting more doubt.

"Nothing, Peaches. Just thought you were more of an outie than an innie." Brona shrugged.

"Don't listen to her, Wanda!" The bird flapped his wings. "You're definitely an explorer."

"Fluffy is right. Don't listen to me. Go ahead." The banshee gave a nod to the door. "Open it."

Wanda hesitated. She wasn't sure what to do.

"You've made up your mind," she told herself.

She stepped up to door number two. She lifted her hand to pull it open—and stopped.

My life depends on this.

She took a deep breath.

Am I really, really sure?

She glanced at Brona, who was busy rubbing her toes.

Wanda wiped her sweaty palms on her pants.

Yes, I'm sure.

She grabbed the handle.

She pulled open the door—and gasped.

"Hello, Princess." A frog hopped out of the chamber and puckered up his wet, slimy lips. "I'm your destiny. It's you and me forever. Kiss me!"

Good Luck with That

"Oh, noooooooo," Wanda groaned.

"Happy to see you, too, Princess," the frog croaked. "Kiss me." A strand of frog spit dribbled from his lips.

"It's the Royal Prince Frog!" Voltaire chirped. "So delighted to see you again."

Wanda knew this frog. The last time she was in the Scary Wood, he had helped her escape Raymunda, and she was very grateful. He could be a bit of a pest, though.

"I'm sorry," she apologized. "I didn't mean to be rude. I was just surprised to see you here. I haven't forgotten that you saved my life."

"Twice," the frog said. "I rescued you twice." He puckered up his big froggy lips. "Kiss me."

"How did you get behind the Door of Destiny?" Wanda asked, ignoring his request.

"Don't know, Princess. One minute, I'm in the middle of lickin' up flies by the pond. Next minute—*whoosh*—I'm sitting here behind door number two. You know what that means, don't you?" The frog stared at her with his big bulgy eyes.

"You're still hungry?" Wanda said.

"You're a riot." The Royal Prince Frog turned to the banshee. "She can be very difficult," he said.

The banshee stretched her legs, then stood. "She's your problem now, Pickle." She rose from the ground and let her appearance flicker to its hideous form for just an instant. "I have a feeling I'll be seeing you soon, Buttercup. Good luck," she said to Wanda, and started to float away.

"Wait!" Wanda called after her. "What does this mean?" She pointed to the frog.

"I just deliver you to the doors, Sweet Pea. The rest is fate." She continued wafting through the trees until she was out of sight.

"You need to stay away from that one." The frog

flicked out his tongue, reeled in a moth, and swallowed it with a noisy gulp. "Stick with me. I'm your future." He belched. "Kiss me."

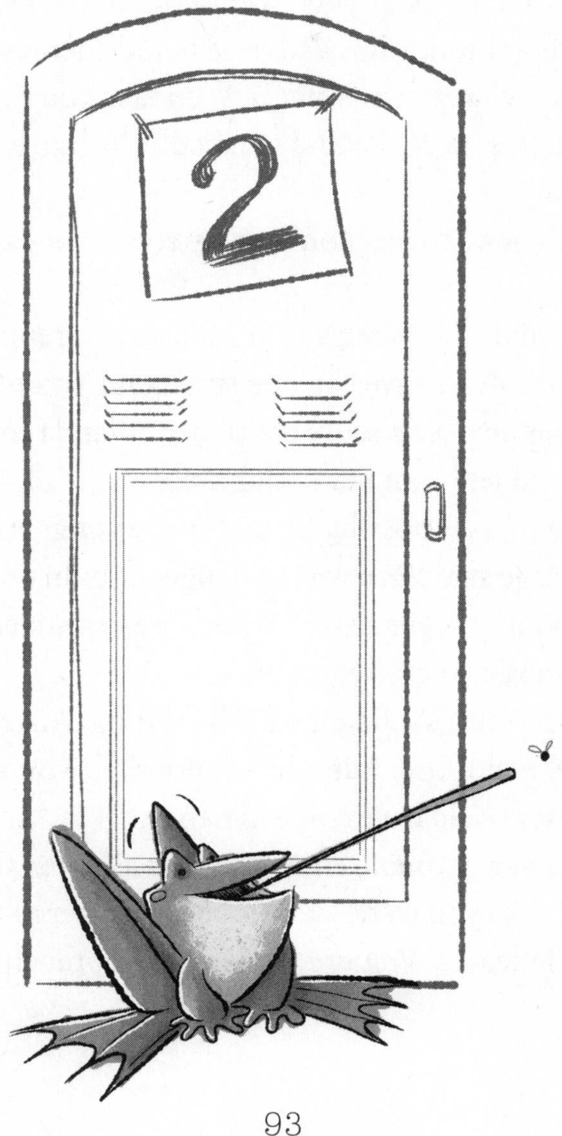

"I'm not going to kiss you," Wanda said. "So please, stop asking."

"But there's magic between us. I can feel it."

"No. I will not kiss you." Wanda stared at his warty skin and his bumpy lips and tried to hide her revulsion.

"I know where your sister is. I can take you there."

"Which sister?" Wanda asked. "Voltaire says I have two."

"That's news to me. I only know about one," the frog replied.

"She might be Wren's twin, but my parents never mentioned her, so we can't be sure. And Voltaire can't remember anything more about her." Wanda frowned. All this suddenly got her to thinking.

"Voltaire, is it possible that you're wrong? After all, the message said *Wren* was in danger. It didn't say anything about another sister." Wanda was confident now that Voltaire was entirely mistaken.

"Good point, Wanda. I *could* be wrong. Anything is possible, I suppose. But what a pity that would be. A spare sister could have come in handy."

"One sister's trouble enough, if you ask me," the frog croaked. "Do you want me to take you to her or not?"

"By all means!" Voltaire flew from the branch he had

perched on and fluttered down to the path. “Lead on, dear sir.”

“Not so fast. Not until I get a kiss.” The frog’s lips parted slowly into a very sly smile. “Kiss me. Kiss me. Kiss me. Kiss me. Kiss me,” he chanted, leaping in a circle around Wanda.

“There will be no kiss. I kissed you once.” Wanda remembered that slimy smooch and cringed. “It didn’t work. I’m not your princess. Please stand still. You’re making me dizzy.”

“But I love you. Marry me.”

“I am definitely *not* going to marry you.” Wanda took a step back from the frog.

“Wanda, a word, please.” The bird turned to the frog. “Pardon us, sir. This will take only a moment.”

“Sure. No problem. I’ll work on the guest list.” He grinned.

Voltaire and Wanda stood behind a tree. “We must find Wren, and the frog can take us to her. This is a bit of luck for us,” Voltaire whispered. “Perhaps you should reconsider his proposal.”

“I’m not getting married. I’m only eleven! And I would never marry a frog,” Wanda protested. She sneaked a peek at the frog, who was trying to swallow a slippery worm. He blinked hard and his huge eyeballs pressed down on his mouth, which helped shove the creature down his throat.

"Blech." Wanda groaned. She took a deep breath. "I'll see if I can persuade him to help us anyway."

"Frog, the witch has my sister and her life is in danger. . . ." Wanda started, using her nicest tone.

"Tell me something I don't know."

She let out an exasperated breath.

"If you won't help me, then won't you please help her?" She patted the frog on his head. Her fingers slid on his mucous-y skin and she couldn't help it—she shuddered.

"You could learn to love me." The frog eyed Wanda as she wiped her hand on her pants.

"Yes! Yes, you could!" Voltaire agreed. "Stranger things have happened!"

The frog's glance darted from Wanda to the bird. "Okay, Princess. I'll take my chances. I think I'll grow on you. Your sister is in the witch's cottage."

"You mean castle," Voltaire chirped.

"No. It's a cottage," the frog said.

"How odd. I was certain it was a castle."

"How do you know she's in a cottage?" Wanda asked, trying to figure out who was right.

"What can I say? You hop around. You hear things." The frog rolled out his tongue to snag a snack and zapped a roach. He swallowed it and smacked his lips. "Mmmm. Crunchy."

"Well, if he says it's a cottage . . ." Voltaire was not totally convinced. But after a moment, when the idea had a chance to take root, he came to accept it. "Fine, sir. We're off, then, to a cottage to bring Wren home."

"Good luck with that." The frog rolled his eyeballs.

"What does *that* mean?" Wanda placed her hands on her hips, trying very hard to remain patient.

"She's under a spell, Princess. She won't go with you."

Bleeding Tooth Fungus

"Voltaire, do you have any idea how to break a spell?" Wanda sighed. "What do you think we'll need?"

"Princess, Princess, Princess. You're asking the wrong guy." The frog hopped closer to Wanda. "What you need is *me* and some bleeding tooth fungus."

"Bleeding tooth fungus?" Wanda glanced at the bird. "Why do I need *that*?" she asked the frog.

"You need the blood to sprinkle on your sister."

"We're going to sprinkle tooth fungus blood on my sister? I don't think so." Wanda had never heard of tooth fungus blood, but it sounded disgusting. She ran her tongue over her teeth to make sure she didn't have it, whatever it was.

"Let me explain." The frog hopped on a log to give his speech. "Bleeding tooth fungus is a type of mushroom. It's white. It looks like a tooth. And it oozes blood." He smiled, very pleased with his presentation.

"Real blood?"

"Not real blood. But it looks like it. And we need the blood. Okay, the not-blood. Whatever. To sprinkle on your sister. It will cure her of the spell she's under. Maybe."

"That's excellent, sir," Voltaire said. "And where would we find this bleeding tooth fungus?"

"I hope it's not in the witches' garden," Wanda said. She'd been to the witches' garden the last time she roamed the Scary Wood. It was a terrible place, and she never wanted to go there again.

"Not the witches' garden." The frog hopped down from the boulder. "It's in the fairy garden."

The fairy garden. Wanda liked the sound of that. What could be better than sparkly pixies with fancy wings and glittery wands, flitting among the flowers? "Where *is* the fairy garden?" she asked.

"Not close," the frog said. "But lucky for you, I can

take you there." He grinned his froggy grin. "What would you do without me, Princess?"

Wanda and the bird trailed the frog as he went around the Doors of Destiny to the forest beyond. On the way she stopped in front of door number one, wondering what lurked behind it. Brona had told her that the doors would lead to either her destiny or her death. She glanced up ahead at the frog hopping through the trees. Which one was he? She had no way of knowing.

Well, she thought, there was no point in dwelling on it now. "Fairies," she said, as she caught up to him. "I'm going to meet real fairies. This will be wonderful."

I Smell Fairies

"Is something wrong?" Wanda asked the frog, who had come to an abrupt and unexpected halt.

"Just taking a break," the frog replied. "How about a kiss? Give me something to live for." He puckered his lips.

Wanda found the frog's attention very annoying. She tried to change the subject. "Prince Frog, have you ever heard anyone tell a lie about me?" Since the frog hopped all around these woods, Wanda thought there was a good chance he had heard something.

"Yes," the frog said. "I have."

"You have?" Voltaire's wings flapped with excitement. "Please tell us!"

"You oughta know. You told it," he said to the bird.

"What?" Wanda and Voltaire both cried out in surprise.

"You said she'd learn to love me. But she won't even give me a cuddle, a snuggle, a little smooch on the ol' kisser." The frog twisted his froggy lips into a sly smile.

"Not funny," Wanda grumbled.

"Lighten up, Princess. I don't know much, but I know true love when I see it." He puckered up again.

"Can't you be serious?" Wanda asked. "Just for a second?"

"What's the point?" He shrugged. When Wanda frowned at him, he gave in. "Okay. Sure. I'll try—later."

They continued along the trail—until the frog stopped again. "I smell fairies," he croaked. Sure enough, a sugary scent wafted toward them. It reminded Wanda of pink cotton candy. With a few steps, the sweetness became so heavy, Wanda could actually taste it. And then the air took on a crystal shimmer as three lovely fairies floated through the trees.

They were about six inches in height, nearly as tall as a teaspoon. One had long, shiny black hair and almond-shaped eyes, and wore a silky gown of aqua and red. Another had mocha skin and violet eyes. Her lavender pixie dress glistened in a shaft of sunlight. The third was slightly shorter than the other two with skin the color of honey. Her warm brown hair hung in a braid to her waist. She twirled through the air in a sparkly blue tutu.

They were all quite beautiful, but it was their wings that made Wanda think she had fallen into a dream. They were lacy and delicate, and when they fluttered, they flickered with points of twinkling light.

Wanda, Voltaire, and the frog stood under a tree in a gray afternoon shadow, but as the elegant creatures circled them, they were set aglow in their silvery gleam.

The fairies were dazzling. Radiant. And Wanda quickly realized that it was impossible to have any bad feelings in their presence. As they flitted around her, her mind was emptied of every single troubling thought. Only good things swirled through her head, and there was simply no room for a notion the least bit unpleasant. She smiled as her thoughts drifted from snowflakes and sand castles to starry nights.

"What are you thinking about?" she asked Voltaire, who wobbled on her shoulder in a heavenly trance.

"Good books and blueberries," he replied.

"I'm thinking about eating flies." The frog licked his lips. "Lots and lots of flies." The thought was so strong, so real, so tasty, he belched.

The fairies circled them one more time, then flew off, sprinkling a ribbon of green fairy dust behind them.

"They're leading us to the garden," the frog said, following the glimmer.

As Wanda trailed after the fairies, thoughts of her sister and their mission returned. She no longer had any doubts about saving Wren. They would find the bleeding tooth fungus and rescue her sister. She was sure of it.

***

The walk was a long one, but when the fairy garden came into view, Wanda knew the trek had been worth it. A golden, shimmery, see-through dome rose above the treetops. Wanda's heart quickened, and she picked up the pace. She arrived just in time to watch the three fairies fly right through the bubble. Where each fairy entered, a small dimple formed, then popped out, leaving the bubble smooth again.

Wanda, Voltaire, and the frog peered through the dome. It covered an enormous garden filled with full, leafy trees, brilliant flowers, delectable fruit, and bushes heavy with berries. A blue stone path zigzagged through all of it.

Wanda slowly pushed her hand into the bubble. It felt squishy, wet, and dry at the same time, and it made her laugh. "Ready?" She didn't wait for the frog or the bird to reply. She stepped through the dome.

Now Wanda could see what was hidden from anyone who peered in from the outside—the garden was sparkling with fairies. They flitted through the flowers, sat on the branches, rested under the caps of red-and-white mushrooms. Their dresses were the colors of jewels in fabrics of gleaming satin and the softest silk.

It was everything a fairy garden should be.

A second later, Voltaire and the frog poked their way through the dome. The frog shook his head as if to clear his sight of all the sparkle. Wanda followed his big bulgy eyes as they took in the flowers left, right, and center. Yellow, pink, and red snapdragons on one side, tall wolf's bane with its deep purple petals on the other, bright orange tiger lilies out in front . . . Then he seemed to zero in on something behind the lilies. "This way, Princess." He led them to the bleeding tooth fungus.

Wanda leaned over the plant for a closer look. "Oooh." It was white and spongy, shaped like a tooth, and fat droplets of dark red liquid bubbled up on its top.

It was a nightmare of a mushroom, and she didn't want to touch it.

"I suggest that you grab it by the stalk," Voltaire said, so that's what she did. Reluctantly, she wrapped her fingers around the stem and plucked it.

"May I help you?" A fairy dressed all in gold swooped down, fluttered in front of Wanda, and waited for a reply.

"I came for this fungus to save my sister," Wanda explained. "I'll just take this small one." She held it up. "It's all I need."

"You don't need that." The fairy reached for it, but Wanda pulled her hand away.

"I really, really *do* need it," Wanda said.

"Oh, but nothing leaves our garden." The fairy tilted her head and gave a small smile.

"Surely you can make an exception just this one time," Voltaire said.

"No exceptions, not this time, not any time," the fairy said brightly.

"But she's a special case, believe me," the frog croaked.

"Everything in this garden is special," the fairy said. "Sorry." Then she yanked the mushroom from Wanda's hand.

Wanda's forehead creased in alarm. She had always

imagined that if fairies were real, they would be extra kind. But this one was rude and a little bit frightening.

"I can tell you're upset," the fairy said. "But trust me—you don't need the fungus. Anyone who enters our garden never needs anything again."

Yowza!

"You're wrong," Wanda said. "I *do* need something. I need *this.*" Wanda reached for the fungus and snatched it from the fairy's grip.

"And now we must leave." Voltaire gave one hard flap of his wings and turned to Wanda. "We must hurry along. Wren awaits." He gave Wanda a nudge.

Wanda stepped around the fairy—and heard a low growl at her feet. She didn't know the frog could make such a threatening sound, but it didn't seem to frighten the fairy at all, who flew in front of Wanda to block her way.

"This is your home now. There's no place you'll be happier," she said.

"She's already very happy," Voltaire said. "She couldn't possibly be happier."

The fairy ignored the bird. "You're worried, aren't you?" she said to Wanda.

"Of course she's worried," the bird replied. "She must find her sister. She's happy but worried. Now step aside and let us go."

"That's not why she's worried," the fairy said. "She's worried because she's afraid she *will* find her sister."

"Hogwash," the bird said.

"Baloney," the frog croaked.

"How did you know that?" Wanda gasped. Wanda hadn't shared that fear with anyone—it was a thought too horrible, too selfish, to say out loud—and she felt deeply guilty just having it.

"She's worried that her parents will ignore her once her sister returns home," the fairy said gaily. "That she won't matter anymore. But mostly she's worried that her parents will love her sister more."

Wanda cringed. But she shouldn't have. It wasn't an unreasonable fear, after all. It was quite likely that her parents would dote on Wren to make up for her terrible years with the witch. And of course that would be the right thing for them to do, Wanda thought. But still, her parents believed Wren was smart and she wasn't. Wanda was certain that once they returned home, her parents would favor Wren and snub her completely.

The fairy's glance remained fixed on Wanda. She knew she had hit upon the truth, and her eyes flickered. "No matter. Everything is good here. We have no troubles." There was a lilt to her words, and they floated in the air like a tender melody. But underneath them, Wanda could detect a river of menace. She tried, once more, to step onto the path . . .

. . . and that's when she heard the low growl again. And she realized it wasn't coming from the frog—it was coming from the tiger lilies that circled her feet.

She watched in terror as their petals opened wide, then wider.

She gasped at the centers, where she saw long, sharp teeth.

Then they leaned over and chomped on her knees.

"OW!" she cried and jumped out of their reach.

The garden flew into a rage. The wolf's bane howled. The snake grass hissed. The lion's tail plant let out a mighty roar. Voltaire flew to the safety of a nearby tree.

"Yowza!" the frog croaked and hurled himself into

the air as the snapdragons burst into flames and tried to roast him.

With a wave of her hand, the fairy set green pixie dust swirling around Wanda. As it settled in her hair, a feeling of calm washed over her. The creases in her brow disappeared. Her shoulders relaxed. Her heart stopped thudding. She had no anguish. No stress. No woes. Nothing plagued or vexed her. She felt utterly serene. Everything was suddenly, completely fine.

"I feel so—so happy," Wanda said.

"Yes, isn't that better?" the fairy replied. "There's no one to help. No one to save. There's nothing to fix. Nothing to learn. Nothing to make better. Nothing to brood over. Not a single favor to give or receive. You don't need to accomplish a thing. All is good here."

Wanda felt light-headed, and a giddy smile formed on her lips.

The plants turned silent. The flames fizzled. The tiger lilies backed off and hid their teeth. Total bliss settled over the girl. She was filled only with warmth and good cheer.

"Wanda." The bird returned to her shoulder. "We have a problem here."

"There is no problem." Wanda smiled at the bird.

"There are no problems." She had fallen into a stupor of utter contentment. Her mouth dropped open and she started to drool.

"Very un-princess-y," the frog croaked.

"There are lots of problems." Voltaire plucked a worm from her hair. "We have to rescue Wren and find the book."

The book? Voltaire had never mentioned a book before, she was quite certain, but she didn't care. "We don't have to do a thing," she said. "Everything's perfect."

"It's not perfect, Princess." The frog's big bulging eyes stared at the girl's legs. At the long green vines that had started to sprout from her ankles. "You're growing roots," he said, as he watched them lodge in the dirt.

"These two are filling your head with all the wrong thoughts." The fairy glared at the bird and the frog. "But no worries. My darning needle will fix that."

"Darning needle?" Wanda echoed, curious.

The fairy waved her shimmery wand, and a turquoise dragonfly soared into view. It was holding a very long black thread.

"I think it's going to sew something. How interesting," Voltaire chirped.

"Interesting, indeed," the fairy said. "We're going to sew up Wanda's eyes and ears so she'll never have to see or listen to you or that frog again. So say something nice." The fairy smiled. "It will be the last thing she hears."

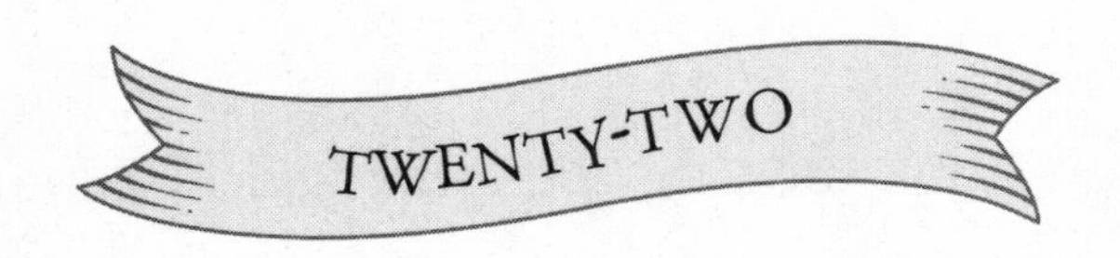

This Won’t Hurt a Bit

KISS ME!” The frog leaped at the dragonfly, trying to stop it, but it casually fluttered out of his range.

“There’s no sense in fighting,” the fairy told Wanda, whose roots now gripped the earth with unusual strength. “This won’t hurt a bit. Just hold still.”

The insect landed on Wanda’s ear.

The frog’s lips parted in a big froggy smile. He opened his mouth and unfurled his tongue. Then, with a confident flick, he reeled in the bug.

He’d never eaten a darning needle before. It was much too salty, and it stuck in his throat. He washed it down with a big gulp of spit.

"Nooo!" the fairy wailed as the frog licked his lips.

The fairy's cry shook Wanda from her fog of contentment. Free of the trance, she snapped her roots.

"Stop!" yelled the fairy as the three took off. "Nothing and no one leaves this garden. Never. Not ever." But this fairy had never, not ever, met the likes of Wanda. With one long leap, she crashed through the bubble. Then she and her friends took off into the woods.

"Well done, Prince Frog!" Voltaire cheered when they stopped to rest. "You helped save Wanda from becoming a bush. What dreadful little creatures those fairies are."

"Yup," the frog grumbled. "They haven't changed a bit."

"Excuse me?" Wanda's voice climbed very high. "You *knew* they were awful? Why didn't you tell us?" Her arms flew up in the air. "Don't you think you should have warned us?"

"You needed the fungus, we got the fungus. Why are you so crabby?" The frog turned to the bird. "I liked her better when she was growing roots."

"You're impossible!" Wanda shook her head in dismay.

"I think she's warming up to me." The frog grinned and leaped back onto the trail. "Come on, Princess. It's time to go rescue your sister—and then we'll get married." His slimy chest swelled with glee. "I can't wait!"

Wanda stared at him as he hopped away.

She thought about the cruel fairy.

She thought about having her eyes and ears sewn up.

She thought about what it would be like to bring Wren home.

She even thought about how absurd it would be to marry a frog.

And with all these things bumping around in her head, she realized later, she completely forgot to ask Voltaire about the book he said they needed to find.

Dead at Last

"Their wings should be plucked!" It was the next morning, and fairies were still very much on Voltaire's mind. He spent the first hour of the day vigorously complaining about them.

As he grumbled on and on, Wanda yawned. She couldn't help it. She hadn't gotten much sleep the night before. They'd found a perfect place to camp out, tucking themselves into a small cave of blue rocks, but the bird had kept them up late into the night, squawking about the small, winged creatures.

"After all, they're half human and half bird," Voltaire lectured, his ruffled feathers standing on end. "A combination of the smartest species on the planet—no offense to you, Prince Frog. And yet, their conduct was atrocious." It was clear he took their bad behavior personally.

"That gold fairy tried to turn me into a plant." Wanda shook off her sleepiness. "I still can't believe it."

"And she attempted to wipe out your memory!" Voltaire huffed. "And rob you of everything that mattered to you!"

Wanda hadn't thought about it that way. For the few moments that she'd been under the fairy's spell, she had felt perfectly happy, but Voltaire was right. The fairy had erased everything important to her, and now, looking back on it, it was a hollow kind of happiness. She remembered the empty feeling that had settled inside her. As if somehow she was missing from her own life, and she didn't like that one bit. "All in all, it's much better to have things to worry about," she said.

"Well, then, you're in luck, Princess. There's Raymunda's cottage." The frog pointed just ahead of them to a dark gray stone house surrounded by trees. "And it looks like she's expecting you."

Wanda studied the cottage. It was slightly smaller

than her house and had a blue slate roof that slanted down toward the door. The door was set back under an arch, but Wanda could see that it was painted a muddy green.

In the front were two large windows made of leaded glass and framed in old splintered wood. The roof had three small windowed gables. The eaves over each one shielded the panes from the sun's cheerful rays. A tall chimney straddled the peak.

An old rocking chair sat on a narrow wooden porch. Even though there was no hint of a breeze, the chair moved ever so slightly, letting out a soft *creak, creak, creak. Eerie,* Wanda thought, and shivered.

No lights on inside. No smoke from the chimney.

"Why do you think she's expecting me?" Wanda asked the frog. "I don't think anyone's home."

"Over there, Princess. On the side of the house," he said.

Wanda's gaze shifted to a small, cleared area.

There appeared to be a long hole in the ground, with dirt piled nearby. It looked like . . . an open grave.

"That's for you," the frog said.

"How do you know *that*?" she asked.

"Oh, he's absolutely correct," Voltaire chirped

from a tree branch above. "From this spot, I can see the gravestone perfectly. It says: HERE LIES WANDA SEASONGOOD. DEAD AT LAST."

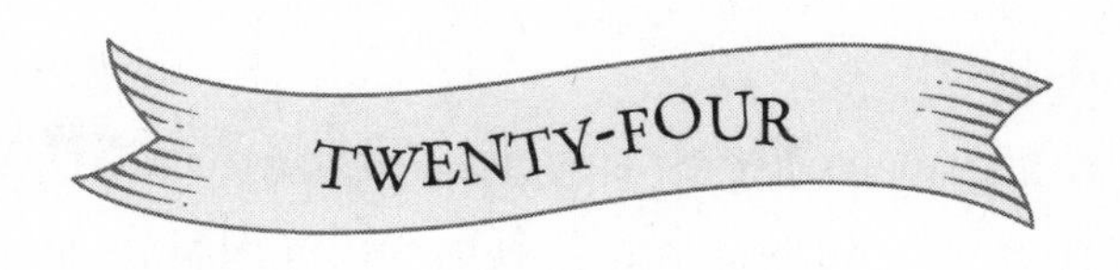

Does That Even Make Sense?

Wanda found it strange to see her name on a tombstone, and stranger still that it didn't upset her. Instead, it ignited her bravery. Her determination to rescue her sister was deeper and wider than any grave a witch could dig. She would battle Raymunda if that's what it would take to bring Wren home. She'd prove to herself and her parents that she was smart and brave, and her victory would have nothing whatsoever to do with luck, as her mother had suggested.

"It will take more than a hole in the ground to stop me," she said. Then the front door opened, and she gasped.

A girl stood in the doorway. "That must be Wren!" Her hair was the same reddish brown color as Wanda's, but Wren's was long and shiny, nothing like Wanda's frizzy nest.

Wren was twelve years old, only a year older than Wanda, but Wanda thought this girl looked at least fifteen. She was taller than Wanda and very thin. She wore a short black skirt, a white top, and black boots. Everything about her was crisp and sleek. Not at all like Wanda. Which is not to say that Wanda had doubts about her own looks. She thought she looked just fine but, perhaps, not as fine as Wren.

As she stared at her sister, Wanda's heart beat faster. She wondered what it would have been like if they had grown up together. *Having a sister means you have a forever best friend. Someone you know you can count on always.*

She thought about the years they had missed being together. But a wave of excitement surged through her as she imagined the times they would share now. Any doubts about bringing her sister home vanished. They belonged together, and nothing should have torn them apart. She was furious at the witch for stealing Wren from her.

"It's her!" Voltaire chirped. "Let's go!" The bird flew down from the branch, but Wanda didn't move.

"There's no time to waste." The bird urged Wanda to follow him, but she remained still.

"We need a plan." Her eyes narrowed as she weighed what they should do next. "We don't know if Raymunda is inside."

"We know what we know! We don't know what we don't know! Therefore, we must go in at once!" the bird replied.

"Does that even make sense?" The frog scratched his head.

"He's very smart. It must," Wanda said.

"Success is at your fingertips." The bird flapped his wings with a great rush of air. "We must seize the moment! You're so close to rescuing your sister! We must be bold! We must do it now!" And with that, the bird took off for the cottage.

Wren stepped out of the doorway. She peered into the trees, left, then right, searching for someone, Wanda guessed, but no one was there. Then she turned and headed back inside. As the door started to close, Voltaire soared straight for it. Wanda's heart flipped as he flew through the narrow opening, just managing to slip inside before the door slammed shut.

"Oh, noooo," she moaned. "Well, we have no choice. We have to go in now." She cautiously peeked in every direction before leaving the safety of the trees.

"Bad idea, Princess," the frog croaked, but Wanda continued for the cottage. "Kiss me! Kiss me!" he said, following closely behind her. "One last kiss before we die."

Wanda ignored him.

"The things I do for love," he muttered.

As Wanda approached the house, she stepped through an icy curtain of air. A *spell surrounds this house,* she thought. It's a warning—proceed at your own risk. She shivered as she walked up the front stairs.

She took a deep breath.

She knocked on the door.

Wren opened it.

Up close, Wanda could see that they had the same hazel eyes, the same spray of freckles.

"I— I— " Wanda hadn't thought about what she'd say, and every word she knew suddenly abandoned her.

"She lost her bird," the frog said. "Maybe you saw him? Blue. Chatty. A little screwy, if you know what I mean."

"Yes. He told me you'd be coming." Wren opened the door wider and let them in. Her tone wasn't exactly warm, but it wasn't chilly, either. A good sign, Wanda decided.

Wanda quickly glanced around the room.

Raymunda wasn't there.

She listened for any sign of noise in the house.

All was quiet.

The room surprised her. It appeared, well, normal. It had a deep blue sofa that faced a fireplace. Two purple velvet chairs. A slate floor. A wood-beamed ceiling. On the left, a staircase led upstairs. All in all, it was a comfortable, homey place. There was no sign that a witch lived there, Wanda thought—until she spotted a cupboard in a far corner. Its shelves were lined with beakers and bottles. Some were filled with cloudy liquids that swirled or bubbled.

"Ah, Wanda." Voltaire flew to her shoulder. "I was just telling Wren all about you."

"You're right about the bird," Wren said to the frog. "He's crazy. He told me that this girl is my sister." She turned to Wanda. "My mother has spoken about you often. She's called you many things—but never my sister." A look of amusement lit her eyes.

"But you *are* my sister!" Wanda said. "I know it's hard to believe. I couldn't believe it myself when I first learned about you."

"You're wrong." Wren shook her head. "I am my mother's only daughter. I know what you're doing." She took a step toward Wanda. "You're trying to trick me into going with you. But it won't work."

"But the witch *isn't* your mother. She kidnapped you from our garden. We *are* sisters." Wanda hadn't considered that Wren wouldn't believe her, and her stomach tied itself into a knot. She had to convince her before Raymunda returned. *How can I get her to see the truth?*

She tugged Wren to a mirror that hung next to the front door. "Look. We have the same color hair, the same eyes, the same freckles."

Wren's gaze moved from her face to Wanda's and back again. Wren's features were delicate, a bit more refined. But there was no denying that the two girls looked alike.

"Come with me," Wanda pleaded. "Raymunda is going to harm you. You're in danger here. Trust me."

"No." Wren stepped away from the mirror. "You're

trying to deceive me. My mother loves me. She would never hurt me."

"She's *not* your mother," Wanda insisted. "She's a dangerous witch, and she'll—" Wanda stopped when she heard footsteps approaching from a room at the back of the house.

Who was it?

"I thought I heard voices." William entered the room.

"Why are you here?" Wren asked him.

"I was looking for Wanda. I wanted to make sure she found you." He smiled.

"Yes, we found Wren, no thanks to you!" Voltaire dove from Wanda's shoulder and beat his wings furiously as he flew in circles around William.

"Why did you leave us?" Wanda demanded.

"William," Wren interrupted, "I didn't know you two were such good friends. Wanda's insisting that she's my sister."

"That's because she is," he said.

"Very funny, William."

"It wasn't meant to be funny," he replied, and there was something about his tone that captured Wren's attention. For once, he sounded sincere.

"Why should I believe you? You're a liar. Even the bird knows it," Wren said.

"He's not lying. He's not lying," Voltaire chirped.

"You don't need to listen to Voltaire—" Wanda started.

"I wouldn't," the frog said.

"Because William is telling the truth," Wanda said. "You *are* my sister. My mother and father—*your* mother and father—told me all about you. There are pictures of you in our house!"

"I don't believe you." Wren shook her head. "You're making all this up."

"She's not. I can prove it." William told her.

"*You* have proof?" Wanda asked, surprised.

"Yes, I do."

"Fine," Wren said to William. "This should be interesting. Show it to me."

What Do You Have to Lose?

At that moment, a tree could have fallen, the walls could have crumbled, an army of trolls could have marched through the room, and the two girls, the bird, and the frog wouldn't have noticed. Such was their focus on William. Except for the soft hissing and bubbling from the beakers in the cupboard, the room was silent. Wanda's breathing grew shallow and her pulse raced, wondering what evidence he was about to offer.

William let out a deep breath. "I can't show it to you."

Wanda's shoulders drooped.

"Young man—" Voltaire was about to sling insults

at the boy, but Wanda held up her hand to stop him. Berating William would accomplish nothing.

"I knew it." Wren laughed. "William, I think that was the flimsiest lie you've ever told."

"It's not a lie," William insisted. "It's something you have to prove for yourself. But first, think about this: Have you ever wondered why the witches never leave the Scary Wood?"

"I never had to wonder," Wren said. "Mother told me why. It's because our spells work best here. The Wood is the source of our strength."

"*That's* a lie," William said. "We don't leave here because we can't."

"I don't believe you," Wren said, but Wanda heard her confidence begin to sag.

"Mother kidnapped you," said William, "and after she did, no witch was able to leave the Wood again. There is a rule among the witches that has been obeyed for hundreds of years: Never bring harm to the children of outsiders. Mother broke that rule when she took you. And a curse was brought down on all of us. We're trapped here."

"That can't be true." Wren shook her head. "I *am* a witch. I can cast spells."

"She's tricked you. It's her magic at work—not yours," he explained. "Go with Wanda. You'll see—*you* will be able to leave the Wood. Because you are *not* a witch."

"Why haven't you told me this before?" Wren's eyes narrowed.

William shrugged. "It was easier not to get between Mother and the things she loves"—he turned to Wanda—"or hates. I try to stay out of her way."

The muscles in Wren's face tightened. Did she recognize the truth in William's words?

"What do you have to lose?" William asked Wren. "Go. Go now, before Mother returns. You'll see. You'll have no problem leaving."

If he can convince her to leave, I will forgive him for every lie he's ever told me, Wanda thought. She would probably forgive him now simply for trying. She held her breath, waiting for Wren's decision, but her sister seemed fixed in place.

"Um, Princess," the frog croaked. "The mushroom."

The fungus!

The spell!

How could I have forgotten?

Wanda fumbled with the straps on her bag.

She quickly took out the bleeding tooth fungus—and

before anyone could guess what she was up to, she held it in front of Wren and shook it. Swung it. Whipped it. She did everything she could to fling its "blood" at her sister.

The droplets flew. They showered Wren's hair and her eyelashes. The red liquid dripped down her cheeks. It splattered her perfectly crisp white blouse.

"What are you doing?" Wren screamed. She wiped the blood from her eyes. She blotted her face with her sleeve. She ran her hands through her hair.

And then something shifted in Wren's expression. Her face relaxed, and her eyes glistened with calmness and clarity.

"Well, let's go," the frog croaked. He took a few hops to the door. "It's now or never."

Wren stepped toward Wanda.

Her lips parted in an awkward smile.

This is it! Wanda thought. *She knows now that we belong together!*

"I choose never," Wren said.

Two Ticks of the Clock

"Never?" Wanda thought she had heard incorrectly.

"Never," Wren said.

Wanda turned to the frog. "Why didn't it work? You said the fungus would break the spell. Why won't she go with me?"

"Maybe she just doesn't like you." He shrugged.

"I'm not going with you because I belong here with my mother." Wren made herself perfectly clear.

"Nonsense," Voltaire said. "You belong with your real parents. They love you more than this witch does. In fact, they love you more than they love Wanda. Just ask her." He gave a satisfied nod, and Wanda sighed.

"I don't trust any of you," Wren said. "And I won't go off with you to prove something that isn't true."

"You're making a serious mistake, Wren," William spoke up. "My mother will turn on you the way she turns on everyone."

"She's *my* mother, too. And she would *never* hurt me. She loves me. I'm closer to her than you'll ever be."

Wanda's brow wrinkled. She had never considered, not for a moment, that Wren might have been happy living here with Raymunda. She had assumed her sister's life was bleak, filled with drudgery and pain. But it was clear that the witch had been kind to her. Which made Wanda wonder—why had the note said Wren was in danger?

William interrupted Wanda's thoughts. "If you're going to stay, I'm warning you, you'd better make sure you never get in the way of what she wants."

"And just what is it you think she wants?" The question came from the open doorway. Raymunda stood there, her cold blue eyes grazing the room, taking in the unexpected gathering.

Wanda's skin heated at the sight of her. Raymunda was tall and regal looking, with long jet-black hair that hung in waves to her waist. Her midnight-blue blouse and pants shimmered under a copper-colored cloak. An aura of evil swirled around her.

Her icy stare came to rest on Wanda. As a young witch, Raymunda had been capable of kindness, William had once told Wanda. But she was selfish, too, always scheming to have more of everything, especially power. Her growing greed soon smothered her goodness, and she became rotten right down to the bone. It was clear she feared nothing, and this set Wanda's heart pounding.

"Wanda, it's nice to see you again." Her voice was as silky as the clothes she wore. "I've been awaiting your return. We have unfinished business to attend to." She smiled.

Voltaire flew to Wanda's shoulder. "Fear not!" he whispered to her as Raymunda's eyes brimmed with hatred. "Prince Frog and I will make sure no harm comes to you!"

A flicker of relief flashed in Wanda's eyes, but it wasn't because of the bird's brave words. It was because she remembered the Enlightener, resting safely in her bag. The locket would protect her from any spell a witch could cast. She clutched the rucksack to her chest and felt instantly calmer.

Raymunda's gaze shifted to Wren's blood-spattered shirt. "Daughter, what happened to you?" The witch's tone became sharp, her glance piercing. "William, what did you do to her?"

"It wasn't him. It was *her*!" Wren pointed at Wanda.

"*You* did this?" the witch asked, her stare turning deadly.

"Yes, she did!" Wren said, swooping forward to grab Wanda.

"Stand back!" The frog hurled himself at Wren—and stopped her the only way he knew how.

"KISS ME!" he cried as he lunged for her lips.

And it worked.

At the sight of the frog's puckered lips soaring toward her, Wren jerked to a halt.

The frog's aim was true, and since a stalled target is much easier to hit than a moving one, his lips met Wren's with a loud *SMACK!*

And then the room turned silent.

As the frog's lips met Wren's, for two ticks of the clock, Wanda thought the world had stopped spinning. Whether that was true or not, everyone in the room would agree that something quite astonishing happened.

It was so unexpected, Raymunda screamed.

Wanda gasped.

William froze.

Voltaire squawked.

They all stared down at the floor.

Wren had turned into a frog.

Half a Girl Is Better Than None

The frog formerly known as Wren looked up at the startled faces hovering above her, but her gaze was distracted by a moth flitting by. She flicked out her tongue, and with one solid *THWACK!* she caught the insect, reeled it in, and slurped it down. She smiled an extremely satisfied smile and burped. It was all too much for Prince Frog.

"My TRUE LOVE!" he cried, nearly fainting from joy. "Sorry, Princess." He turned to Wanda. "Wedding's off. I'm going to marry your sister instead." He snuggled up next to his new sweetheart.

"My daughter is not going to marry a frog." Raymunda gathered herself and tried to reclaim control.

"She's not your daughter," Voltaire said. "She's Wanda's sister."

Raymunda paid him no mind. "William, your spell is not amusing." The witch glared at her son. "Turn your sister back into a girl."

"Sorry, but I can't do that." His head tilted slightly as he stared at Frog Wren. "It wasn't my spell."

"Don't lie to me," Raymunda warned him. "I'm already angry with you for filling Wanda's head with nonsense about Wren." She glanced down at Frog Wren, then shifted her gaze to Wanda. "She's *not* your sister."

"She *is* my sister," Wanda said. "And William didn't tell me that. I already knew it." Wanda straightened her shoulders. "One of you needs to change her back into a girl. Right. Now."

"Are you trying to command *me*?" The veins in Raymunda's neck throbbed with fury. Wanda felt the witch's gaze devour her. She was looking for the Enlightener, Wanda knew. Any attempt Raymunda made to hurt her would fail so long as Wanda possessed the charm.

"Wanda, only the one who cast this spell on Wren can remove it." William tried to distract his mother.

"But you witches have extraordinary powers," Wanda said. "Surely you can reverse it."

"One needs to know the exact hex when trying to undo it. Otherwise"—William took a breath—"Wren could become a bit twisted. Unsightly."

"I'll fix this." Raymunda's cold eyes narrowed. "It's just a foolish little spell." She glared at William and raised her wand. "And if something goes wrong"—she shrugged—"half a girl is better than none."

"Leave my sister alone!" Wanda cried out. "Go!" she ordered the frogs, and they took off, hopping out the door.

"Come back here!" Raymunda demanded, but they were already heading into the trees.

"I won't let you hurt her," Wanda declared.

"I'll find Wren, then end you." The witch grabbed Wanda's wrist, yanking her close. "You won't always have my locket to protect you. You'll be careless with it. Stupid girls like you always are."

"I AM NOT STUPID!" Wanda wrenched free. "Why wait to kill me? If you're so powerful, do it now," she said, indignant and angry.

"Wanda, no!" Voltaire's wings beat in a frenzied flutter.

"It's very tempting," the witch replied. Her lips parted in a grin that would make a corpse shiver. "But I'd prefer you have nightmares about it first. And I'd want Wren to watch. It will be a good lesson for her." She turned to her son. "If I were you, William, I'd stop wasting time on silly pranks. You should be practicing ways to protect yourself—from me."

"I told you—I didn't turn her into a frog. But if I were *you*, Mother, I'd worry about who did. It looks like whoever it is knows what you're up to. The book will be useless to you now."

"Yes! Yes! The book!" Voltaire chirped. "Is it here?" He flew from Wanda's shoulder, searching from corner to corner.

"How does he know about the book?" Raymunda's eyes flared with anger.

"Good question," William said, watching the bird dart about the room.

"Voltaire, what book are you looking for?" Wanda asked.

"I will tell you, Wanda, just as soon as I find it." He continued the hunt.

"What is this book, and why is it so important?" she asked William. "What does it have to do with Wren?"

"Do *not* tell her." Raymunda raised her wand, and it turned an icy shade of blue.

"I'm not afraid of you, Mother." His eyes challenged her to strike him. She couldn't resist his dare and took aim at her son. She smiled coldly as the wand's blue tip deepened and blazed.

"No!" Wanda leaped in front of William. She knew the Enlightener would protect her.

"Stop!" Voltaire squawked. "Don't risk your life for him! He's a swindler, a fraud, a liar, and a cheat!"

Voltaire was right, of course. William was all those things. But it was impossible for Wanda to step aside. She simply was incapable of holding a grudge.

She spread her arms wide to guard him.

A bolt of blue lightning shot from the wand. And then William did something swift and startling—he grabbed Wanda's arm and shoved her to the floor.

Before Wanda could sort out why, the icy spike struck him. His whole body trembled. But the bolt bounced off his chest and hurtled across the room. It hit the mirror, shattering it to pieces.

Raymunda's face broke into a smile. Her eyes gleamed with malice and joy. "You really *are* stupid. You gave William the Enlightener." She pointed her wand at Wanda, who was sprawled on the floor. "What an excellent day this has turned out to be. I never imagined I'd be filling your grave so easily. This is going to be such fun."

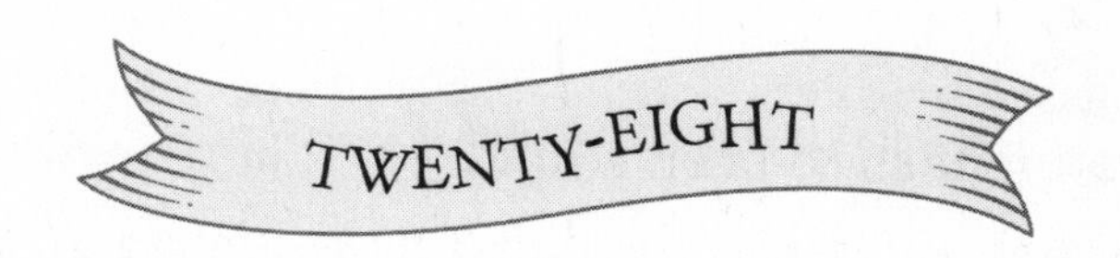

Look Who I Found!

"You stole the Enlightener from me?" Wanda opened her rucksack, which was on the floor next to her, and searched through it frantically.

"He's a thief! He's a thief!" Voltaire cried out.

"Yes, I am," William said matter-of-factly. "I took it from you the other night," he said to Wanda. "When I reached into your bag for your cheese sandwich, there it was. I couldn't resist it."

He turned to Raymunda. "You see? I *am* taking steps to protect myself." He smiled, delighted that he had outwitted his mother, which wasn't an easy thing to do.

Wanda was furious. Although she didn't believe for

one moment she'd been stupid—William's evil was to blame here, not her—she didn't like giving Raymunda any reason to gloat. She was also hurt. *I will never put my faith in that boy again*, she vowed. *Never ever.*

Most of all, though, now that she didn't have any protection against witches, she was frightened.

"Enough chitchat. I'll deal with you later," Raymunda told her son. "Don't spoil this moment for me." She turned to Wanda. "I don't think I'll wait for Wren after all." She lifted her wand and aimed it at Wanda's chest. "I'm going to stop your heart. Slowly. So I can savor the panic in your eyes. It will be so satisfying to watch your lips and skin turn blue. The color of death, my favorite."

"Wait!" William shouted. "If you leave her alone . . . I'll find the book for you."

He steals from me, then tries to save me? Wanda didn't understand.

"How touching." Raymunda lowered her arm. "But I already have the book. In fact, Zane knows it's here. He comes by to look for it whenever we're out. He thinks he's shrewd, but I always know when he's been spying."

"Zane is wrong. If you had the book, you would have used it by now. And besides"—he flashed her a grin—"I know where it is."

"I don't believe you." Raymunda studied William.

"Your loss," said William with a shrug.

"Here's what we'll do," Raymunda finally said. "Deliver the book to me by sunset, and I'll let her live." She glared at Wanda with her frosty blue eyes. "But if you fail . . ."

"I won't disappoint you," William said. He walked out the door, and Raymunda moved to the window to observe which path he was taking into the trees.

Wanda's heartbeat steadied. Her breath became even. William would return with this book and rescue her.

But as she got up from the floor, her mind lit with the horrible truth.

He's bluffing.

He doesn't know where this book is.

He has no intention of coming back.

He cares for no one but himself. In the end, William is loyal only to William. He had proven this to her more than once.

"Voltaire, we can't wait until sunset. We must escape now," she whispered, eyeing Raymunda, who was still looking out the window. "But I don't see how . . ."

"No worries there, Wanda. I will create a diversion so you can run." And before they could discuss his scheme further, he zoomed off.

"I found the book! I found the book!" Voltaire squawked. He began to flap wildly around the room. He crashed into a lamp. Careened into a vase. Knocked over two candlesticks that fell with a clatter. "Here it is! Here it is!"

"Stop it!" Raymunda whirled to face him. "Are you insane?"

Wanda ran to the door. Voltaire's crazy antics were going to work.

She was nearly out . . . when the witch pointed her wand to the floor.

Wanda watched, mesmerized, as the shattered pieces of mirror began to rise.

A ray of white light shot from the wand's tip, and the glass shards floated up to meet it. The pieces melted into the light, which grew so bright Wanda had to squint.

Voltaire, unaware of the sorcery, headed toward the bubbling, hissing bottles in the cupboard.

The witch took aim at him.

The blinding beam illuminated his feathers.

"No!" Wanda jumped into its path.

"Eeeeiiii!" she cried out as the white-hot ray hit her legs. Her skin began to tingle. Then it turned frigid. And then she felt absolutely nothing at all.

She looked down—and gasped. Her legs had transformed into two glass mirrors. She saw her stunned face in each of them.

"Excellent! This will do nicely. Take one step and your legs will shatter." Raymunda headed to the door. "Now, I must go see what William is up to." She glanced out the window. "Not to worry. I'll be back." She gave a wicked smile. "And there'll be no one here to protect you," she added and left.

The bird landed at Wanda's feet. "I will reflect on a solution for our current crisis." He stared at himself in her mirrors. All that flapping about and bumping into things had ruffled him up quite a bit. He started to smooth his feathers.

Wanda stared down at her legs. Her breath was shallow. Not a muscle twitched. She tried very hard not to blink. She knew that one wobble, one jiggle, one off-balance wriggle could bring her crashing down, with her legs smashing to pieces.

"I'm done for," she said.

"Done for? Nonsense, dear Wanda. While I've been tidying up, I've been thinking. These woods are filled with witches, and I will find one to break this spell!"

"I don't think . . ." Wanda started, but the bird had already flown out the door.

"Wait!" Wanda called. Too late. She could see him through the front window now, heading into the woods.

How will he know where to look for witches?

Will any of them be willing to come to my aid?

Her next worry was sharper and bit at her nerves.

What if they hurt him?

But as often happens, the things we fret over aren't where our troubles lie. In less than five minutes, Voltaire had returned.

"Wanda! Look who I found!"

"Oh, nooo," she moaned.

She couldn't think of anyone worse to help her.

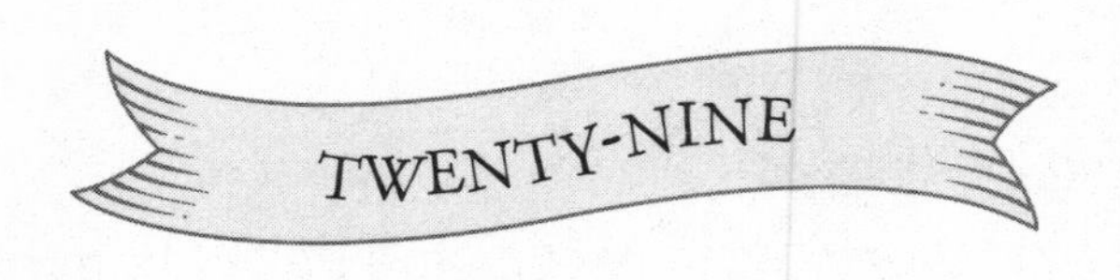

I Can't Believe We Didn't Think of This Before

Zane.

Tall, handsome, and very cruel Zane.

He swept his coal-black hair from his eyes. They were the same shade of blue as William's, but while William's gaze was pleasant, Zane's was stony.

"Wanda. What a surprise. Why are you here? Did you miss me?" He sneered.

Wanda thought it best not to answer.

He walked around her, studying her legs. "I guess you bumped into my mother." He laughed. "Mirrors. I wonder what would happen if they were to break."

"I'll tell you what would happen, young man!" Voltaire flew in front of him and cut off his path. "Seven years of bad luck, that's what! And look at her—Wanda certainly doesn't need any more of that! You must use your magic to reverse this spell!"

Zane was so much more wicked than Raymunda. His mother hurt people to gain power or get revenge. But Zane didn't need any reason at all. He found delight in the misery of others, and his happiness swelled when he was the cause of it. Wanda was already in great danger, and she knew her problems would triple if Zane stayed.

"I don't need your help. Really," Wanda said. "I'm fine."

"Wanda, you are many things, but fine isn't one of them." The bird shook his head. "She most definitely needs your assistance."

"I never help anyone . . ." Zane started, and Wanda was relieved. She simply wanted him to go.

"Then again . . ." He smiled. "You did free me from my mother's spell. I suppose I owe you for that. And it will make my mother very angry if I meddle with you."

"Then meddle away," Voltaire encouraged him.

"No! Really! It's not necessary. . . ." Wanda protested.

But Zane had already lifted his wand. It looked very different from the other wands Wanda had seen. William's was made of dark brown wood. Raymunda's was jet-black. But Zane's had a golden glow to it. He caught her staring at it.

"It's made from the wood of the yew. A tree with poisonous seeds." He flicked it lightly and smiled. "Perfect, don't you think?" Then he snapped it harder, and aimed for her legs.

"Very good!" Voltaire chirped as he watched the tip of the wand glow orange. "Progress at last. Wanda, you'll be changed in no time!"

A wave of dizziness washed over her. What kind of spell was he going to cast? She didn't have to wonder for long—her legs began to itch. She wanted to lift them. Scratch them. But she didn't dare move.

"Zane, what are you doing?" She tried to hide her fear.

"Helping you." He grinned, and the itching stopped. But her feet began to tingle and grow warm. Too warm.

Her breath turned into short, frightened gasps. "Maybe—maybe you should stop helping me."

"Don't listen to her," Voltaire instructed. "In fact, could you work a little faster? We have so much to do!"

"No, no! I think you should stop." Her knees were turning boiling hot. "I think my legs are on fire."

"Excellent. Just as the spell requires." Zane gave a satisfied nod and headed for the stairs. "Is Wren here?"

"Ow, no," Wanda replied. "Ow, ow, ow." She groaned in pain.

"Perfect." He started up the steps.

"Zane . . ." Wanda called, but he didn't answer. He continued up the stairs—probably to search for the book, Wanda thought.

"Dear me." Voltaire stared at Wanda's mirror legs, which had started to drip. "I think you're melting."

"Voltaire, that grave outside won't be empty for long. I'm afraid this is the end." Wanda's heart pounded as she peered at the silvery puddle forming at her feet.

"Oh, but you are greatly mistaken, Wanda. 'Now this is not the end. It is not even the beginning of the end. But it is, perhaps, the end of the beginning.' Winston Churchill said that, and it couldn't be truer here. . . ." He hopped happily around her feet. "Because I can see your real legs. They were hidden inside the glass. And now that the mirrors have trickled away—well, there they are!"

Wanda looked down. "You're right! I see them, too!" She let out a long, happy, relieved sigh.

When the last of the glass had slipped from her legs, she and Voltaire wasted no time. She flexed her knees—they felt strong and solid—and she and the bird bolted from the house and headed for the shelter of the trees.

"We have to find Prince Frog and Wren." She stopped to catch her breath. "And someone who can help us turn Wren back into a girl."

"Very good, Wanda. I'll go fetch Zane." He started back to the cottage.

"No! Stop! Come back! We need to find someone else!"

The bird returned. He lowered his head and started to pace the forest floor. Wanda always knew when he was thinking hard. The trickiest problems required the most steps. As he walked back and forth, he covered a rather large area for his little bird legs.

"Wanda!" He halted and took a joyful leap into the air. "I know exactly where we should go! It's so obvious. So logical. So clearly correct! I can't believe we didn't think of this before!"

End of Story

The All-Knowing Phyllis. We will go see her at once!" Voltaire flew to Wanda's shoulder.

The All-Knowing Phyllis.

The fortune-teller who lived in the Scary Wood.

Of course.

She lived deep in the trees, off a path not usually traveled. She wasn't like the other residents of the Wood, who were extremely dangerous or downright deadly, Wanda thought. Still, there was something not quite right about her. But the fortune-teller had helped them the last time they were there, and that was good enough for Wanda.

"The All-Knowing Phyllis will tell us who put the

curse on Wren," Voltaire said. "Then we will find that person and insist they remove it. And your slimy green sister will be a girl again!'

"Voltaire, this is such an excellent idea. You're a genius!" Wanda said. "But first, we have to find Prince Frog and Wren."

"Hello, Princess! Look no further. Here we are!" With one long leap, Prince Frog jumped over a shrub. Frog Wren emerged from the bush and joined him.

"What are you two doing here?" Wanda asked. "Why aren't you hiding somewhere safe?"

"I was waiting for you." The frog licked his lips. "Kiss me. Kiss. Me." He puckered up.

"Kiss you? Why should I kiss you?" Wanda asked. "You've already found true love." She glanced over at her slick, bulgy-eyed sister.

"It's not true love. I was wrong." The frog shrugged, then hopped closer to Wanda. "You don't really know someone till you've lived with them," he whispered.

"But you've been with her for less than an hour," Wanda said.

"It's enough. All she does is eat flies and belch."

"But that's all you do," Voltaire noted.

"In case you haven't noticed, bub, I talk. She doesn't. End of story. I'm not marrying her."

"We're going off to find the All-Knowing Phyllis." Wanda returned to their immediate dilemma. "She'll tell us how to cure Wren. I think you should wait for us in the hidden blue cave. You'll be safe there."

"Will do, Princess. And while you're gone, I'll study the calendar and pick a date for our wedding. Are there any days that won't work for you?"

"Prince Frog, I hope you'll still help us, but I need to make something perfectly clear." Wanda did not want to leave the frog with the wrong impression. "I am never going to marry you," she said firmly.

"Sure you are. Just ask the fortune-teller. She knows everything about everything." The frog grinned his big froggy grin—and a wad of frog phlegm flew from his lips. "It's you and me together. That's what she'll tell you. Till death do us part."

* * *

"There it is." Wanda rounded a curve in the woods and stopped. The path they were on led right to the door of the fortune-teller's old shack. It was tucked into a stand of trees, and it was made of the same wood, which kept it well camouflaged.

Even though Wanda had been here before, she shuddered at the structure's tumbledown state. Its planks were still rotting and gouged. There wasn't much left of the covered porch—just a few crumbling floorboards and a wooden railing, splintered and leaning low over the dirt. The front had no windows. If the shack held secrets, they were safe from anyone inclined to snoop.

Wanda and Voltaire stepped up to the door, which looked like it had been slashed with a knife. And there were fresh gashes in the cabin's walls, too, probably made with a very sharp ax.

"Voltaire, I'm amazed we found the cabin so easily." She tried to put herself at ease. "At least for once, something is going right." She raised her hand and knocked on the door.

"Hello?"

No one answered.

Wanda knocked again.

What if Phyllis isn't home?

What if she doesn't live here anymore?

Wanda's pulse started to pound.

What would they do if they couldn't find her?

She knocked one more time.

"Hello? It's me. Wanda."

"I know that." A voice came from inside, and Wanda's heart slowed to a normal beat. "Why wouldn't I know that? I know everything. I knew you were coming before you even knew you were coming."

Wanda smiled. Phyllis would help them, and Wren would be saved. "Sorry, you're right," Wanda said.

"Apology accepted," the fortune-teller replied. "Now do me a favor."

"Of course," Wanda said.

"Go away and never come back."

Three Questions

Go away? That wasn't at all what Wanda had expected to hear. She stared at the door in surprised silence. Voltaire's reaction was quite different.

"Go away?" he said. "Nonsense. We'll do nothing of the sort. So you might as well let us in."

"I knew you'd say that." Phyllis yanked open the door with a loud *screech*. "It's the same thing every day: Phyllis, tell me my future. Phyllis, tell me what I need to know. Blah, blah, blah. No one ever leaves me alone." The fortune-teller's voice grew louder as she complained.

"So what do I do? I don't answer the door. I chop up the walls of my shack to make the place look scary. They come anyway. Just like you." She shook her head. "Well, don't just stand there." She pulled Wanda inside.

Upon seeing Phyllis, a sensible person would have promptly fled. She was old and hunched, and she loomed above Wanda the way a vulture hangs over its prey. Her wrinkly brown skin sagged from her high, full

cheekbones. On each side of her head, tufts of brittle black hair stood straight out, resembling the whisks of a broom.

She wore bright pink lipstick—her favorite color, Wanda guessed, because it matched her bright pink shirt perfectly.

The most frightening thing about her right now, though, was the large hammer she held in her hand. "Don't move." She raised it high . . . and slammed in a nail sticking out of the wall beside Wanda's head. It happened so quickly, Wanda barely had time to gasp.

"Thought I'd straighten up for you. I hate a messy house." She waved the hammer toward the table and chairs in the middle of the room. "Go sit."

Wanda's knees wobbled as she took a seat. She gazed around the room. It looked just as she remembered. There was a shabby couch slouched against one wall. An old refrigerator, stove, and sink lined another. Unlit candle stubs sat on a small table in front of an armchair. Though the weather was warm outside, Wanda wished there were a fire in the fireplace because of a definite chill in the air.

"Are you ready?" the fortune-teller asked, sitting across from Wanda.

Wanda was wondering if they should leave. The-All-Knowing Phyllis seemed a little stranger than the last time they'd met, but the fortune-teller didn't wait for Wanda to reply.

"I am the All-Knowing Phyllis," she began. Her voice turned low and mysterious. "Look into my eyes. I can see what is to be seen. I can tell what is to be told. Most of the time. And never on Tuesdays. Is today Tuesday?"

"What luck!" Voltaire chirped. "Today is *not* Tuesday!" He flew to Wanda's shoulder, fluffed his feathers, and settled in.

"Shouldn't you know what day it is?" Wanda asked. "You're supposed to know everything."

"Why should I know what day it is? Today is the present. Tomorrow is the future," the All-Knowing Phyllis said. "I do the future. You want to know about tomorrow? Ask away."

"Makes perfect sense," the bird agreed.

Wanda didn't think it made sense at all, but she was eager to see if Phyllis could help them, so she didn't dwell on it.

"I'm ready," Wanda said. She stared into Phyllis's startling black eyes. They were so large and shiny, she could see herself reflected in each of the glassy, dark pupils.

"I am the All-Knowing Phyllis," the fortune-teller started again.

"Sorry to barge in," Voltaire chirped, "but it might be helpful for you to know that we're looking specifically for information about Wren, Wanda's sister. She's been turned into a frog."

"It's not helpful at all. Stop interrupting." The fortune-teller focused her gaze on Wanda. She stared deeply into her eyes. "I see— Hmm. I see two sisters."

"*Two* sisters! I knew it!" Voltaire hopped up and down. "I knew I was right!"

Two sisters. Wanda shook her head. *I never should have doubted him.* "I know where one sister is," she said. "We found her in the witch's cottage. Can you tell me where the other one is?"

Phyllis squinted as she gazed into Wanda's eyes. "Well . . . it looks like . . . a castle."

"A cottage *and* a castle! That's why I saw both! You have a sister in each place!" Voltaire chirped. "My mind is as sharp as ever!"

"Is it the giant's castle?" Wanda's stomach twisted into a very tight knot.

"Could be. Who knows?" Phyllis stared hard into Wanda's eyes. "Wait. No. Don't think so."

Wanda asked Phyllis to tell her more about this sister in a castle. But the fortune-teller couldn't come up with anything else. "Do you see a frog?" Wanda prompted, hoping to learn something more about Wren.

"I *do*. How odd." Phyllis's eyes narrowed. "I see a frog and a wedding."

"Oh, nooo," Wanda moaned.

"And a book," Phyllis said.

"The witch's book!" Voltaire bounced up and down.

"No." Phyllis shook her head. "It's not the witch's book. It's *Wanda's*."

"Wanda! You've written a book! How thrilling! Now I can quote you, too!"

"That's very nice of you to say, Voltaire, but I haven't written a book. I think she means it belongs to me. Are you sure it's *my* book," Wanda asked, "and not the witch's?"

"Of course I'm sure," Phyllis replied. "I'm thirty percent accurate one hundred percent of the time."

"But that means you're wrong more than you're right," Wanda pointed out.

"You're very judgmental." Phyllis shrugged.

Wanda was extremely disappointed. Yes, they had learned important news about her other sister. And about the mysterious book, which now puzzled Wanda more than ever. But first and foremost, she needed to know how to cure Wren, and on this item they hadn't made one bit of progress.

"Not to complain," she said to Phyllis, "but I thought you'd be able to tell us who turned my sister into a frog. . . ."

"And how to turn her back again. I know. I know," Phyllis said. "I wasn't finished yet."

"Sorry," Wanda said. "I'm just a little anxious."

"I knew that, too," Phyllis replied. She pulled her chair in closer to the table. "Now, look into my eyes, and I will learn what there is to be learned."

Phyllis's eyes were dark mesmerizing pools of black, and Wanda stared deeply into them.

"That's better," the fortune-teller said. "Let's see. . . . You have three questions. When you find the answer to one, you'll have the answers to the other two."

"How exciting!" Voltaire chirped. "You're going to find the answers to your questions at last!"

"*Three* questions?" Wanda scratched her head. "What are my three questions?"

"*You're* supposed to know the questions. *I'm* supposed to know the answers. Don't you understand how this goes?" Phyllis turned up her hands.

“Sorry,” Wanda said. “But I’m still not clear on the questions.”

“Fine.” Phyllis blew out a frustrated breath. “Here are the three things you’re wondering about. Your sister,” Phyllis started and Wanda nodded.

“The book.”

“Yes, indeed,” said Voltaire.

“And the key to every strange thing that has happened to you and will happen still,” Phyllis said. “The lie.”

But What's a Pooka?

The lie! How could I have forgotten about the lie? Wanda couldn't fathom how it had slipped her mind.

But *how* was actually quite understandable. With Wren changing into a frog and Wanda's legs turning to glass and William deceiving her at every turn—how many problems could she possibly ferry all at the same time?

"Where can I find the answers I'm searching for?" Wanda asked. "Can you look into my eyes and see?"

"Been there, done that. Nothing there," Phyllis said. "You'll have to find out by yourself."

"But where do I start?" Wanda asked. "We thought coming here would help us. Not that you haven't helped us," she quickly added. She didn't want the fortune-teller to think she was complaining again.

"Complaining again." The All-Knowing Phyllis shook her head. "Want to know what I do with people who annoy me?"

"Oh, yes. By all means," Voltaire chirped.

"No, you don't." She shook her head. "You're lucky. I like you. You won't ever have to find out. Now . . . let's get back to your problem. Go see the pooka. You'll be surprised at how much he knows about you. He'll definitely, most likely, probably agree to help you. At least, I think so. Depends."

"Depends on what?" Wanda asked.

"Depends on whether he's in a good mood or not," Phyllis replied.

"I'm sure he'll be delighted to see us and in a very good mood because of it!" Voltaire chirped.

"What exactly is a pooka, anyway?" Wanda had never heard of one before.

"He's a little gray hairy thing with a long tail," Phyllis answered. "Except when he's not. He's a shape-shifter. He could look like anything—a horse, dog, rabbit, human . . . anything."

"Then how will we know we've found him?" Wanda asked.

"Good question," the All-Knowing Phyllis replied. "A very good question."

Wanda sighed. "This will be impossible. We don't know what he'll be—a rabbit, a dog, who knows what. And we don't know the first place to look for him."

"Of course we know *where* to look for him," the fortune-teller said. "I never said we didn't know *where*. I just said it was a good question."

"Hope is alive!" Voltaire cheered. "Tell us where we might find this chap, and we will set off swiftly!"

"Go into the woods behind my cottage," Phyllis instructed. "Walk until you come to the quiet stream and the golden ragwort that grows next to it. You can't miss the ragwort's flowers—they're bright yellow."

Phyllis stood and went to a cabinet over the sink. The rusty hinges let out a sharp and stinging squeal as she opened it. Wanda wondered when she had last looked inside there. "Aha! Here it is!" Phyllis rummaged around old dusty jars and pulled out a wrinkled, withered, brown paper bag tucked way in the back. "Eat what's inside this, and the pooka will appear." She handed the bag to Wanda.

The bag was the size of a lunch sack, so Wanda was surprised at how heavy it was. She started to peek inside.

"Don't open it!" Phyllis warned her. "Don't open it

until you're ready to eat it. And when you do eat it—you have to eat all of it. ALL. OF. IT. Every last morsel. It will taste disgusting. But you have to eat something repulsive for the pooka to show up." She headed for the door. "Sorry to rush you, but if you want to find him, it's time for you to leave. Love you. Miss you. Ta-ta. Hate to see you go."

Wanda sprang up from the chair, smiling. She didn't have her answers yet, but she was certain she would. "I think Voltaire is right," she said. "I have a feeling the pooka will be in a very good mood!"

"Oh, I doubt that," the fortune-teller muttered to herself in the doorway. "Nasty, probably. Bloodthirsty, possibly. But in a good mood? Not likely. Not likely at all."

Astound Yourself

"We should have stayed with Phyllis. Just for the night." Wanda shivered in the damp evening breeze. She wasn't one to become easily frightened, but the evil of the Scary Wood grew stronger at night. The air was thick with it.

I think we're being followed. Every few steps she jerked to a stop, gazing into the darkness. She froze at the sight of the trembling shadows. *Just branches swaying in the mist,* she realized as she swept her flashlight through the trees.

"I can't see very much with this small light," she said, aiming the beam on one side of the path, then the other.

"No need to fret about that," Voltaire said, hitching a

ride on top of her head. “I have excellent eyesight.” He fluffed his feathers and nestled down into her frizzy hair.

“It was so exciting to hear about your other sister,” he started to chat. “I knew she was in a castle! So, first we will free Wren from her froggy form. Then we will find this other sister and the fellow who has her.”

The fellow who has her?

Voltaire never mentioned a fellow before, had he?

Wanda searched her memory, which was much easier to navigate than the bird’s. No, she was sure. He had mentioned that her sisters might be twins, but he had never said anything about a fellow.

“What do you know about this fellow?” Wanda tried to keep her voice light and cheerful. An urgent tone, she feared, might make the bird nervous and forgetful.

“Let me see. . . . Ah, yes,” Voltaire chirped. “He’s a witch.”

A witch. Of course.

One of Raymunda’s sons? There were lots of witches in the forest.

“Voltaire, might it have been William or Zane?”

“William or Zane? William or Zane?” The bird flew from the top of her head. As she lit his path with her beam, he began pacing the ground in front of her. “William or Zane?” Walking always helped him concentrate. But this time, he evidently needed to think very hard because he walked and walked . . . until he walked straight out of sight. And just when she was about to call for him to come back, he shouted, "Wanda! Success!"

She followed his voice and found him on the other side of a thick shrub next to a quiet stream. Wanda could see the water's soft ripples in the hazy moonlight. Tufts of flowers grew along its bank. Only the morning would prove if they were truly yellow, but Wanda was certain that they had found the right spot.

"It is time to summon the pooka!" Voltaire declared.

Wanda plopped right down on the ground and unbuckled her rucksack. She took out the brown paper bag and, in one swift move, opened it, then crushed it shut. "It smells disgusting." She began to choke from the stench.

She took a deep breath and tried again. "Ewww," she groaned as she peered inside—at the solid brown lump in the bag. "It looks like . . . it looks like . . ." Wanda didn't want to say.

She opened the bag a little wider, and the food—if it could be called that—began to stretch. Voltaire peeked inside the bag. "Wanda, dear, it looks like your dinner is waking up."

Then the clump started to shimmy. The bag grew warm. The clump got smellier.

"Like rotten eggs and the most awful fish." Wanda gagged.

"All righty!" Voltaire chirped. "It's time to eat!"

"Voltaire . . . I don't think I can. I don't even want to

touch it," she said as she reached into the bag. She broke off the tiniest piece of the stinking lump. Her stomach lurched.

"I couldn't possibly put this in my mouth." She shook her head. "I've done many things I never dreamed I'd do in these woods, but I just can't do this."

"Oh, but you're wrong. 'If we did all the things we are capable of doing, we would literally astound ourselves.' Another wise saying from Thomas Edison. Wanda, it is time to astound yourself!"

Wanda stared at the putrid little chunk in her hand.

She brought the piece to her mouth.

"It might not taste as bad as it smells," she tried to convince herself.

She took a small bite.

It was part chalky. Part wet. And she was right—it didn't taste as bad as it smelled. It tasted much, much worse.

Anyone else would have stopped there and then. But Wanda was determined to astound herself. She broke the chunk into three large pieces, held her nose, and forced each down her throat in three giant gulps.

Then she held her stomach and groaned. "I wonder how long it will take for the pooka to show up."

She waited and waited, but he didn't appear. She

gazed into the shadows, willing him to come. Her back straightened at each snap of a twig, each crunch of a leaf.

The pooka has to come. He just has to, Wanda thought. *I need his help to save my sister. And I must win my parents' respect. I will never have a chance like this one to change their minds about me.*

Two hours passed, and there was still no sign of him.

She stared into the empty bag. "I ate every last morsel." She sighed. "Why isn't he here?"

A Rock Might Make an Excellent Friend

Wanda vowed to stay awake all night to wait for the pooka's arrival, but soon her head began to droop and her eyelids slid shut. When she woke up the next morning, a dark gray, growling beast stood over her.

It was a wolf. His upper lip curled back, and she gasped at the sight of his slick, sharp teeth. He let out a snarl, and a hot strand of drool landed on her cheek.

She jumped up—and the wolf sprang forward. "Nooo!" she hollered as he flew at her. She leaped back and slammed hard against a tree.

Voltaire returned from gathering berries. "Wanda!" he shouted. "How splendid! The pooka is here!"

"Splendid?" the wolf growled. "I'm bloodthirsty and nasty and in a very bad mood. You should be afraid of me. Very afraid."

"But we thought you would help us," Wanda said, her voice slightly shaky.

"Everyone wants something for nothing these days." With a loud *POP!* the wolf changed into a scraggly, gray, hairy thing with huge pointy ears, shifty green eyes, and a once fluffy tail that was now mostly chewed up. He resembled a very large rabbit gone wrong. "What took you so long to get here, anyway?" he grumbled.

"Excuse me?" Wanda asked, surprised. "We came straight to this spot from the fortune-teller. It didn't take us long at all."

"No. No. No." The pooka let out a long, impatient breath. It smelled foul and fusty, and Wanda leaned away. "I dropped that rock on your head days ago. Then I made a stone trail for you to follow. It's been days, I say. Days!"

"*You* dropped that rock?" Wanda asked.

"Those were *your* stones?" asked Voltaire.

"Yes, I did. And yes, they were."

"I can't believe it." Wanda shook her head.

With a squeaky *POP!* the pooka turned into a fly. "Does this seem familiar?" he asked. "When you looked up to see where the rock had come from, all you saw was me. You were so confused—I just loved that." He chuckled.

Wanda didn't think it was funny, but she was relieved that his mood had improved. With another *POP!* he changed back into the sort-of rabbit.

"We tried to follow your stones, but you turned them to ash," Wanda protested.

"You should have moved faster." He shrugged. "Everyone takes their own sweet time these days."

"That wasn't very nice," Wanda said. "We tried to get here as quickly as we could."

"That's your problem, not mine. I have my own troubles," the pooka complained. "The witches can't leave the woods, so I'm their messenger. It's 'take this here' and 'take that there' all day long." He stomped the ground with a big, fuzzy foot, and that's when Wanda noticed all the stones that surrounded them. Stones just like the one that had hit her on the head. Piles and piles of them.

"I love rocks," he said, following her gaze. "They don't cheat, lie, or steal. They do exactly as they should. They'll never disappoint you."

"How true," Voltaire agreed. "You know, I hadn't considered this before, but a rock might make an excellent friend."

"I don't think it would be very good company," Wanda said, staring at the stones. Then her mind suddenly flashed with an exciting thought. "Pooka, did you send that message to me?"

"No, I didn't," he said. "And before you ask"—he sighed loudly—"I can't tell you who did."

"Why not?" she asked.

"It's against the Pooka Pledge."

"What's that?" she asked.

"*That* is a secret." He crossed his long, scraggly arms in front of him. "I *can* give you a clue, though. That's what we do—pookas give clues. But do I want to? I don't have to, you know."

He studied her with his creepy green eyes, trying to decide. "You seem all right," he finally said. "Not as nice as a rock, but then who is?" He headed down a path behind Wanda. "Turn around and come with me." He shook his head. "Nobody follows instructions these days."

They stopped in front of an extremely big stone that had an extremely long sword wedged into it. Its silver handle looked tarnished and ancient.

"Wanda! This is excellent," Voltaire chirped. "A magical sword! If you can pull it out of the rock, you will be its rightful owner, and its powers will be yours!"

Wanda stepped up to the sword.

She wrapped both hands around its hilt.

She took a deep breath, pulled with all her might . . . and the sword came flying out of the stone. Still gripping it tightly, she landed on her backside in the dirt. "I did it!" she said. "I pulled it out!"

"Of course you did." The pooka shook his head. "Anyone can pull that rusty old thing out. You don't need the sword. You need the rock."

"The rock? Why?" Wanda asked, disappointed. She tossed the rusty sword aside.

The pooka didn't reply. With a very loud *POP!* he turned himself into an inky-black goat with two giant curved horns.

"No need to thank me. Nobody thanks anyone anymore these days," he said. "Keep your eyes open for clues." Then he stood up on his two hind legs and walked away. It was a very strange sight to behold, but oddly enough, probably not as strange, Wanda thought, as a girl and a bird staring at a rock, waiting to see what it would do.

An Impossible Clue

"Wait!" Wanda called out to the pooka. "Why do I need this rock? Does it talk? How will it help us?" But the goat continued on his way without giving them another glance.

"Voltaire, what do you think?"

The bluebird hovered above the stone. "No clues from up here," he said, then he landed on top of it. He lowered his head to study it closely. He pecked at it with his beak. "How unusual," he said. "It appears to be an ordinary rock. But the pooka said it holds a clue, and so it must. Therefore, I know exactly what we should do."

At times like these, Wanda was tremendously grateful

to have such a wise friend. She waited patiently for him to go on.

"We will return to Prince Frog and Frog Wren to make sure they are safe. We will take the rock with us, and perhaps, along the way, it will reveal itself to us."

Wanda studied the boulder. It was about the size of a beach ball but ten thousand times heavier. "Voltaire, I couldn't possibly carry this rock."

"I totally agree," he said, and Wanda sighed with relief. "That is why I suggest that you push it."

Push it?

There must be a better way, Wanda thought. But when nothing else came to mind, she realized Voltaire was probably right. She leaned over, placed her hands on the stone—and pushed. And pushed. With a loud groan, she pushed again. The rock didn't budge.

"Try with your feet," the bird suggested. So Wanda sat down on the trail, planted her palms in the dirt, brought her feet up to the rock, and pushed again.

"That's it!" Voltaire cheered when the rock moved one half of an inch.

Now that the boulder had been loosened from the earth, Wanda discovered that she could move it with her hands. "This is going to take forever." She grunted as she nudged the rock along the path. On either side of her, the ground sloped downward, so she was careful to bump the stone along in the middle of the trail, inch by difficult inch.

"Why couldn't it have been the sword instead of the stone?" Wanda grumbled. "Why couldn't that pooka have helped us instead of leaving us an impossible clue?" Her hands were gritty, her forehead damp, and she was very, very unhappy. How could shoving this rock possibly help her find Wren? She imagined her parents' disappointed looks when she returned home without her sister. Her heart sank and her frustration swelled.

"A troll, a giant, a gruesome thumb. Fungus and fairies and too many frogs," she muttered under her breath. "And now I'm pushing a big, dirty rock." Her voice grew louder. "All for a sister I probably won't even like."

"I couldn't have said it better myself!" Voltaire chirped.

Exasperated, she gave the rock a serious shove—and watched in horror as it tilted and rolled off the path.

"No, no, no!" she cried out as it tumbled down, down, down to a ditch below. It only stopped when it became wedged between two trees. "Now what will we do?" she moaned. Voltaire flew to the base of the hill to study this new dilemma.

"I'll never be able to push that rock back up here," Wanda called to him as he landed in front of it.

"Not to worry," Voltaire chirped. "You won't have to. Events have progressed according to plan. The clue has revealed itself! Come down and see!"

The Book

Voltaire, what do you think it means?" A message was written in curvy black letters on the bottom of the rock.

The pen is mightier than the sword.

"It's a wonderful quote from the writer Sir Edward Bulwer-Lytton. It means that if you want to change people's minds, words are more powerful than weapons. And how true it is," Voltaire chirped.

"I know that," Wanda said, sitting down next to the rock. "But there must be more to it. The pooka said it's a clue."

The pen is mightier than the sword.

Wanda thought about the sword she had pulled from the rock. But that didn't help. *What am I missing here?* she wondered.

"Oh!" She leaped up. "I've got it!"

She flung open her rucksack and dumped everything out. "Here it is!" She picked up the old, tarnished pen that the pooka had dropped on her head. She stared at the big-horned goat on its top, which she had forgotten all about. She looked into the goat's silvery eyes—then snatched up her diary and started to doodle.

Voltaire watched closely as her scribbles turned into . . . a map!

"Well done, Wanda." The bird flapped his wings. "It's showing us the way to a castle!"

"But I thought that was where my *other* sister was." Wanda shook her head. "What about Wren? We have to change her back into a girl."

"We will save this sister first and without regret. You'll probably like her better anyway! Besides, the message is clear. We must go to the castle."

* * *

"We found it! We found it!" Voltaire hopped up and down on Wanda's shoulder. "That's the castle!" It wasn't as big as the giant's, but it was grand nonetheless, with an extremely large turret on one side.

"I've definitely been here before!" Voltaire chirped. "I remember it now! When I was winging my way to your house, I stopped to rest on the branches of this tree." He pointed above their heads. This is where I heard the fellow talking about your other sister and the book—and the lie as well! It's as clear to me as a starlit sky on a slightly cloudy night."

"That's fantastic!" Wanda said. "What did you hear? Who was speaking? Tell me!"

"I will!" he chirped. "Once we're inside, I will most likely remember all of it!"

Wanda had a great deal of faith in the bird's lost-and-found memory. But it was hard to wait for everything to come flooding back to him.

She stared up at the castle. Who lives here? she wondered. Was this Zane's home? Or William's? She realized she had no idea where either one of them lived. It was time to find out.

"Let's sneak in over there." She spotted a window near the ground, and as luck would have it, it was partially open. She swung her legs over the frame and landed inside with a heavy thud. The moment her feet touched the floor, the window slammed shut. Was it witch trickery? Wanda thought so, and she started to shiver.

She studied the room. It was filled with dust-covered boxes, brittle newspapers, and musty old clothes, all stacked behind bars. Bars! She quickly realized she had dropped into a dungeon.

She made her way around the piles of junk to the cell door. She held her breath and pushed. It swung open with a sharp *shrieeek*, and she sighed with relief.

The bird perched on her shoulder as they entered a dark, chilly corridor lit by a few grimy, sputtering torches. The air down here was stagnant and stenchy, and she tried not to breathe.

She peeked into each cell they passed—and froze when someone stepped out of the next one they reached.

"Look who's here." It was William. "I see you escaped my mother's clutches and followed me." He nodded approvingly.

"I did *not* follow you," Wanda said. "I'm searching for my sister."

"Why are *you* lurking about in the dark?" Voltaire asked.

"Do you live here?" Wanda asked.

"No, I don't. But the book does," William replied. He turned and took a book from the cell. Wanda could see it had a brown leather cover, but she couldn't read the title in the dim light.

"What *is* that book?" Wanda asked. "You have to tell me."

"Of course I will. It's an ancient book of spells and charms," he said. "Its pages hold the secrets of the universe—how to change the path of the planets, shift the oceans' tides, live forever, revive the dead, create

riches beyond one's wildest dreams. It would corrupt even the most honest witch, if there is such a thing. It is too powerful for any one person to possess. My mother craves it. My brother craves it more. Its spells are more powerful than anything a witch can conjure, even Exemplaries. But—"

William would have gone on if it weren't for the footsteps they heard coming from the end of the hall. A tall man stepped from the shadows into a dim circle of light.

"Gadzooks! There he is—the fellow I told you about!" Voltaire whispered. "I remember him now! He is the witch who has your other sister!"

Wanda pressed herself against the wall. She narrowed her eyes to try to get a better glimpse of the man. He was tall, with brown hair, and a manner about him that seemed calm and gentle. “He doesn’t appear the least bit dangerous.”

The man stared into the darkness but didn’t see them.

“He’s not dangerous at all,” William said, watching him leave.

“Are you sure?” Wanda asked. She had learned not to trust anyone in the Scary Wood. Especially witches. But there was something about this man that looked familiar. She had a strange feeling they had met before.

“I’m very sure,” William said. “His name is Zell. He’s my father.”

The Other Sister

"Your father?" This news gave Wanda a sudden jolt. "You never mentioned your father before. I—I—thought he was dead."

"We pretend that he is." William laughed. "My mother hates him because he's not like us. He's good."

"Good? I find that hard to believe." Voltaire shook his head. "I will spy on this man to see if it's true." The bird took off but returned just a few moments later.

"I saw her! I saw her!" His feathers fluffed with excitement. "Your other sister *is* here! Excellent for sure—except for one small concern. I'm sorry to report that you probably won't like her. She's Wren's identical twin!"

"You *do* have another sister?" William said, surprised. "And she's here with my father? I would never have guessed."

"Another Wren." Wanda shook her head in dismay.

"Another Wren!" The bird gave a small hop. "Let's go and meet her!" He led Wanda and William up the steps so they could see this twin for themselves.

Wanda walked into the room and gasped. She stood in an enormous library with gleaming wood shelves lining every inch of each wall. The books were covered in luxurious leather. The titles were printed in gold. Each tome was a treasure. If she had to spend the rest of her life in one room only, it would be this one.

Her glance roamed the library, searching for her sister. She saw windows draped in rich gray velvet. A midnight-blue ceiling that sparkled with stars. Polished wood tables. A pale gray sofa with a back so high, it would hide anyone who sat there. And, finally, seated in a chair off to the side, she saw Wren's twin, staring out the window, lost in her thoughts.

"Hello. I'm Wanda. I—I'm your sister."

The girl turned to Wanda. "I know. Zell told me you'd be coming." She sounded and looked *exactly* like Wren, and even though Voltaire had told Wanda that she was an identical twin, Wanda was still astonished. "I still can't believe you're my sister," the girl said, sounding slightly bewildered.

"Wanda! You're here! And William. I wasn't expecting you, too." Zell entered the room. His deep blue shirt set off his light cocoa skin. He had William's chiseled good looks. His eyes were an extraordinary shade of violet, and they twinkled as he gazed at Wanda. "Wanda, it's nice to see that you still love books."

He knows me, Wanda thought, but as hard as she tried, she couldn't remember a time when they'd met.

"And I'm very happy that you found my pen helpful."

"*You* sent the pen?"

"Yes. With the pooka's assistance, I sent it to you so you could get here quickly, before any harm could come to your sister."

"I'm afraid it's too late for that, sir," Voltaire chirped. "I regret to inform you that Wren has been turned into a frog."

"No regrets necessary. That frog isn't Wren," Zell said. "That frog is a frog. I bewitched it to look just like Wren and to behave as Raymunda would expect."

No wonder the bleeding tooth fungus didn't work, Wanda thought.

"It was a wonderful spell, if I must say so myself," Zell

continued. "But the real Wren, as you see"—he pointed to the girl in the chair—"I have safely hidden here."

"I should have guessed it." Raymunda stood in the doorway, her appearance a surprise to all. "Your dull game is over. I'll take my daughter home now."

Wren jumped up from her chair and glanced at Zell, her stare a bit frosty. "He says you're not my mother. I don't know who to believe."

"Wren, please be patient. You'll have your proof soon enough," Zell replied, then he turned to his wife. "Ray, so nice to see you! It's been a long time." He smiled. "But I'm afraid my 'dull game,' as you call it, has just begun."

"How lovely! A family reunion," Voltaire chirped. "While you two catch up, we'll be on our way. Wanda, Wren, it's time to leave." He nudged Wanda's head with his beak, then turned to William. "Please give Wanda her book."

Wanda still didn't understand why this book should be hers. Just the same, she wondered if William would surrender it.

He slipped it out from under his vest. She could read the title now. It was called simply *The Book*, as if once you owned this one, there would be no need for another.

William reached out . . . to give the book to his father. But as it traveled from hand to hand, Raymunda snatched it. She didn't grab it firmly, though, and it fell to the floor.

Wanda watched as the pages fluttered in the air before the book landed.

She let out a sigh wrapped in deep melancholy. *William has done it again.*

This could not be the book he had told her about.

The pages were blank.

Boiled and Fizzled

Why did you lie?" Wanda asked William. "There isn't a single word written on those pages."

"He isn't lying. At least not this time." Raymunda picked up the book and swept her fingers over its cover. "Wren is the only one who can read it. That's why it's *her* book, not yours, which means that it's mine." She took Wren by the arm and started to leave.

"Before you go, let Wren look at the book." Zell suggested. "Let her read a spell or two."

Raymunda's forehead twitched. She carefully handed the book to Wren. The girl opened it to the middle. Her eyes remained fixed on the pages. She turned to the beginning, then to the end. She lifted her gaze in confusion. "I don't understand," she said. "There's nothing to see."

"That's impossible!" Raymunda shouted. "She's the one! I know she is!"

Zell took the book from Wren and gave it to Wanda. Her heart skipped a beat as she felt it grow warm in her hands.

She opened it. The pages were blank . . . and then they weren't. She watched as handwritten curves faded in, then out, then in again, as if it were no small task to make themselves seen. But finally letters appeared and words became whole and Wanda could read them completely. On this page, they described in the utmost detail how to turn house dust to diamonds, and it was easier than one might expect.

"How is this possible? I'm not a witch, am I?" Surprised, she snapped the book shut. "How is it that *I* can read this?"

"You're lying!" Raymunda shouted at her. "You don't see a thing. You're making it up." She pointed her wand at Wanda, and the tip blazed a wicked green.

"No!" William shouted.

"Put that wand down!" Zell glared at Raymunda.

"Wanda does not lie," Voltaire squawked, and before anyone could stop him, he soared at Raymunda.

With a quick flick of her wrist, Raymunda aimed the wand at the bird. There was a spark and a *BANG!*—and Voltaire plummeted to the floor like a rock.

Wanda stared at his limp body, and her heart practically stopped. Her face grew pale. "He's not moving." Her voice came out in a whisper. "You've killed him." Tears filled her eyes. She stared in horror at his once blue feathers, now a drab shade of yellow. At his swollen body. At a face that was no longer his. He remained stone still. She lifted him gently from the floor.

"I turned him into a chicken," Raymunda sneered. "Fare is fowl, and fowl is fare. For once, he'll be useful. We'll eat him to celebrate. Right after I lower your body into your grave."

Then, with a gleeful shriek, she aimed her wand at Wanda. But Zell was swifter than his wife—and he blasted the girl with a white-hot bolt.

Wanda's eyes grew wide with shock. Her bones twitched and sizzled. Her blood boiled and fizzled. She knew this is what it would feel like it if she were hit by lightning. She closed her eyes tightly and opened them only when the buzzing stopped.

When her lids fluttered open, she was still holding Voltaire and the book. Wren was right beside her. But they stood in front of the Doors of Destiny. Zell had sent them there, she realized, to save their lives.

"Hi, Hon." As Wanda tossed the book into her bag, Brona the banshee came out of the trees and floated toward them. The scent of lilies swirled in the air.

"Oh, nooo," Wanda moaned. "Have you come to take Voltaire away?" She stared at the dead, fat chicken in her arms.

"Not today, Toots." Brona straightened her bright paisley shift. "He'll be fine. Just give him a minute. You'll see."

"Who is she?" Wren stared at the barefoot woman whose feet remained floating above the ground.

"I'm Brona, Sugar Pie. I'm in charge of dead things and destiny in the Scary Wood. But your sister has the book now, so that puts her in charge of me."

The banshee reached into her pocket. "Congrats on retrieving the book. I brought you a present," she said to Wanda. She held up the dead man's eye. "Give it a look-see. You can thank me later—when it shows what you need to know about the lie."

Beats Me, Baby Cakes

"The lie?" Voltaire finally raised his head and let out a cluck, capturing Wanda's attention. "Did someone say something about the lie?"

Wanda gave him a hug. "Voltaire, I'm so happy you're alive!" She smoothed out his feathers.

"As am I!" He cocked his head to one side. "But I appear to be a chicken. Would that be correct?"

"I'm afraid so," Wanda said

"Hmm. A chicken. Not a rooster," Voltaire mused.

"Raymunda's sense of humor, I guess." Wanda frowned.

"Do not fret, my dear girl. As the wonderful novelist Charlotte Brontë said, 'I try to avoid looking forward or backward, and try to keep looking upward.' A positive attitude will carry us far. I'm a chicken," he crowed. "And who knows—the change might do me some good!" And with that he lifted his wings, launched from the girl's arms—and plunged straight down into the dirt.

"Haven't you ever seen a chicken?" Wren couldn't help but laugh. It was a charming, joyful laugh, Wanda thought. *I think we're going to have great fun together.*

"Chickens can't fly." Wren smiled at Voltaire.

"Evidently," said the bird, brushing himself off. "Therefore, upon further reflection, I think I'd prefer to be myself again. But I'm curious about one small thing. Before we attempt to reverse this fowl curse, I would like to try to lay an egg."

"Can we stop talking about chickens?" Wren's smile faded. "Wanda, you and Zell say I'm your sister. This is all so confusing. Where is the proof he promised? And what's the lie you're talking about?"

"The lie is the key to every strange thing that has happened to Wanda and will happen still," Brona said. "And it's your proof, Lambie."

The banshee held out the dead man's eye. "You'll see the answers here."

Wanda gazed into the glistening eye and grew instantly dizzy. Her head started spinning, her heart began pounding, and she suddenly felt like a pinwheel caught in a storm. But just as she was about to turn away, it all stopped . . . and she saw herself and her sister in the depths of the eye. . . .

She and Wren were home, playing in their garden. She was three and Wren was four. Wren skipped down a white stone path in a bright yellow dress. Wanda sat under a tree, looking at the pictures in her favorite book. She glanced up from the pages to see a young boy, Zane, race into their arbor, ripping out flowers and eating dirt. From the wild look in his eyes, it appeared he was under some kind of curse.

And now there was Zell! He stepped out from behind a tree. He smiled at Wanda. Then he pointed his wand at her and began to chant as he cast a spell.

Wanda stared off for a moment, wishing she could hear what was being said. But she turned her attention back to the eye when she spotted someone new. . . .

There was William. Crouching . . . hiding behind a shrub . . . watching his father. He stayed there until his father left, then stood when Raymunda came into view. They spoke—oh, how Wanda wished she could hear their words—*then Raymunda took young Wren's hand, and off the three of them went. . . .*

The eye became cloudy. Wanda waited for something new to appear. Something that would help her make sense of what she had seen.

"I remember that dress. And the garden. And that path," Wren murmured in disbelief. "That was my

home." Her shoulders slumped with sudden exhaustion. "I remember you," she said to Wanda.

The two watched the eye grow dark. It had nothing more to reveal.

"Wait! What does it mean?" Wanda asked Brona.

"Beats me, Baby Cakes." She tucked the eye back into her pocket. "Ask him." Brona gave a nod to the trees, where William was making his way toward them. "He can explain."

FORTY

The Almost Perfect Lie

"William, why did you take me away from my home?" Wren demanded. "We saw it in the dead man's eye."

"Yes," Wanda said. "We saw it all. What kind of spell did your father cast?"

"And no lies, young man!" Voltaire warned.

"No lies," William pledged, placing a hand over his heart. "At least for now." He laughed, but no one gave him even the slightest smile.

"All right then," he said. "But we should walk while I tell you. That's why I'm here—to lead you to the edge of the forest before Mother finds you." So the three bid

Brona a hasty goodbye and quickly took off, with Wanda carrying Voltaire in her arms.

"The day Zane ran into your garden," William started, "my father had much on his mind. He had hidden the book, but he was still worried that somehow my mother or brother might find it."

Wanda shuddered at the thought of the book in either of their hands.

"My father had already put a spell on my mother to weaken her powers. He was going to do the same to Zane. But when he reached their cottage, he saw that Mother was one step ahead of him. She had already cursed Zane. Except her magic was frail and Zane was strong, and her spell didn't quite work. She had turned him into something half beast, half boy, and he ran away. We found him in your yard. We didn't know that Father had followed us there."

"Well, now at least we know why everyone was in our garden," Wanda said.

"My father saw you reading," William continued, "and suddenly he had an idea. He would enchant you, so you would be the only one who could read his book. If it was stolen, he reasoned, the pages would appear blank. He thought his idea very clever."

"One moment, please." Voltaire gazed at the sisters. "Why should we believe any of this? Pledge or not, this scoundrel never sticks to the facts."

"This is the truth," William declared. "Although there *is* a lie—but it comes a bit later." He grinned, pleased at the thought.

"As I said, my father thought he was being quite crafty," William continued. "No one would guess that this ordinary girl, living in an unremarkable house with an average family, would be the key to something so powerful."

"Hold on! Ordinary girl? Is that what you said?" Voltaire ruffled his feathers. "Don't you know, young man, that everything you say should be true, but not everything true should be said? Please keep that in mind when you speak of our Wanda."

"What about the lie?" Wanda ignored the bird, anxious for William to get to that part of the story.

"My father headed back to the woods. Then the rest happened so quickly. My mother said we were leaving Zane behind. And she was going to take you with us instead. There was something about you she liked. That's when I told her the lie."

William let out a long breath. Wanda inhaled deeply.

Wren stopped breathing altogether, waiting for William to finish.

"I told my mother about my father's spell—but I said Wren was the one he had enchanted. I lied. I knew about the book's power. My father had warned me that it must never be used by my mother or brother. I thought I needed to protect it and Wanda.

"It would have been a perfect lie, too. But a few weeks ago, Mother started searching for the book—so I confessed to my father what I had done. He feared for Wren's safety. He thought that if my mother discovered Wren couldn't read the book, she might kill her. But he told me he'd take care of everything, and he sent me on my way."

"So he switched me with a frog and summoned you to rescue me," Wren said to Wanda. She shook her head in despair. "All these years, I've been living the wrong life. All these years, it should have been you. *You* should have been the one taken."

Wanda stood silent, trying to make sense of it all. Every question about her strange life had finally been answered, which should have made her feel better, and it did, but she felt worse, too. A single lie had changed both their lives completely.

"Here we are." William stopped. They had arrived at

the edge of the forest. "My mother is probably nearby. You need to leave now." He held out his hands. "Give me the chicken."

"Excuse me?" Wanda cleared her mind to focus on Voltaire. She clutched him closely.

William moved toward her.

Wanda stepped back.

William reached out for the bird. "He shouldn't go home until I reverse the curse. And, since I wasn't the one who cast the spell, I need to take my time. With a bird, even a small mistake could have grave consequences."

Wanda hesitated.

Should she trust the boy? He was a liar, a thief, and above all, a witch, and she couldn't be sure what he really might do. So she thought about it hard and sincerely. Then she loosened her grip on the bird. Voltaire was meant to fly. It was, she decided, worth the risk.

"I'll be watching you very closely, young man," the bird said as William started to carry him away. "Be warned. I may not have teeth, but I have a very sharp tongue."

"I'm so happy this little episode is over," William said, turning to enter the Scary Wood's deep shadows. "I'm tired of telling the truth. I hope I never have to do it again."

I'd Rather Have a Frog for a Sister

I'd rather have a frog for a sister.

Wanda felt bad thinking that, but Wren refused to speak to her the entire way home. Not a word, not a nod, not a blink or a smile. With a frog, at least there'd be hopping and leaping and a fine talent for slurping. And as far as Wanda could tell, frogs were hardly, if ever, in a bad mood.

The more she tried to talk about the shocking things they had just learned, the angrier Wren looked. *All these unexpected events have unnerved her. She just needs time to adjust to the facts,* Wanda guessed. *I know I do.*

She stopped trying to talk to her sister and thought

about *The Book* instead. She couldn't wait to read its secrets.

And she thought about her parents. She had done it—she had survived the Scary Wood again—and she would tell them all about it. And they would have to see how clever and courageous she was. And they would love and value her.

She glanced over at Wren. *Once she's back where she belongs, she'll be happy I rescued her.* Wanda smiled, thinking about how much better both their lives would be.

* * *

"Wren! It's Wren!" Mr. and Mrs. Seasongood opened the front door just as Wanda and Wren stepped onto the walk that led to their house. It was a happy coincidence, and a wonderful welcome home for her sister, it seemed, but Wren's gaze remained hard.

The Seasongoods flew from the porch and wrapped Wren in a circle of hugs. Then they glanced Wanda's way. "Wanda! We're so proud of you!" Tears streamed from her mother's worried eyes.

"Now we're finally the family we were meant to be." Her father gave them his sunniest smile.

Still, Wren didn't utter a word.

She must be scared, Wanda thought. *We're practically strangers to her, after all. She doesn't really know us.*

When they were seated in the living room, Wanda told her parents all about her frightening yet excellent adventure, and even though her parents were amazed that she had actually rescued her sister and were, indeed, impressed and grateful, they could not keep their eyes off Wren. And Wanda understood completely. It was only natural that they would be preoccupied with Wren's return, she told herself. *As soon as they're accustomed to having her back, everything will be fine. Meanwhile, I'll give them some time together,* Wanda decided and headed upstairs to her room.

She plopped down on her soft, comfy mattress and wrapped herself in her cushy quilt. She was so happy—tonight she wouldn't have to sleep on the cold, hard ground.

Her gaze traveled the room to take in the things she loved. There was her desk and her pens. Her shelves spilling over with books. The tree outside her window with its nests and nooks that she knew by heart. She took off her shoes and ran her toes through her plush purple carpet. Her room was hers alone. It was where she did her best thinking. It was her favorite place to be.

She opened her rucksack and took out *The Book*. She wasn't sure what she was supposed to do with it—besides keep it safe, that is. She wondered what would happen if she tried one of the spells. She wished Zell had told her more.

As she started to open it, she heard her parents and Wren approaching the stairs. *I'd better hide this.* She quickly leaped up from the bed.

She dove for her closet and removed two floorboards way in the back. *No one will ever find it here.* She slipped it under her diaries, replaced the planks, and covered them with a pile of notebooks and a mound of shoes. Then she leaped onto her bed, pretending she had never been anywhere else.

She heard her parents giving Wren a tour of the house.

"And this is Wanda's room." The three had made it to Wanda's end of the hallway. She looked up to see them standing in her doorway. "We'll fix up your room any way you'd like," her mother said to Wren.

"We don't have to bother fixing my room. Wanda said I could have hers. It's perfect." Wren's lips curled into a sly smile. "I'm very lucky that she's my sister."

"Yes, you are," her parents agreed. "And Wanda is very lucky to have you."

In a miraculous show of self-restraint, Wanda held back the words that stormed her mind. Most of them weren't the least bit polite, and none of them had anything whatsoever to do with being lucky.

Dear Dwana

Wanda sat on her front porch, searching the sky for Voltaire. It had been three days since she had last seen him. She missed him terribly. He was her only friend, and a friend was what she truly needed right now.

Wren had taken over the household. She complained about everything—the soup was too cold. Her room was too hot. Her chair was too hard. Her bed was too soft.

Wanda's fear that her parents would be consumed with Wren and would ignore her completely had come true. But Wanda wasn't upset. It wasn't because her parents loved Wren more or respected Wanda less. It was simply because they were overwhelmed with Wren's demands, and Wanda felt sorry for them. They had refused to let Wren have her room, and for that alone she was very grateful.

Wanda had tried to talk to her sister, but Wren had made it very clear: Wanda was the one who should have been kidnapped. Now she, and everyone else it seemed, would have to suffer for it. Wanda tried to tell her sister how awful her life had been living with Zane, and it truly had been, but Wren would hear none of it.

Every morning, Wanda woke up eager to look at the book hidden in her closet. She wondered if she had to be a witch to cast its spells. But Wren was always hovering nearby, and she couldn't find a safe time to put herself to the test. *As soon as Voltaire returns, we will find a private place to read it together,* she thought.

Her mind drifted to William. He could teach her about the spells. Would she ever gaze into his handsome face again? He was a liar and a thief, but there were times when he had tried to protect her. He had inherited some of his father's goodness, she realized. Sometimes he acted with honor, sometimes with evil. It was so hard to know which William he'd be. She wondered if it was confusing for him as well.

Would he help her again if she were in need? She liked to think so—but she knew she couldn't stake her life on it.

And then there was the Royal Prince Frog. Wanda smiled. He was a pest for sure. Stubborn. Single-minded. And extremely slimy. But he was a very admirable creature. Just the same, it didn't look like he was her destiny *or* her death, and about this she was much relieved.

Voltaire was her main concern, though.

Where *was* he? She knew that a million things could have gone wrong when William attempted to reverse the curse.

She imagined a bluebird with the head of a chicken. Or a chicken with Voltaire's short, spindly legs. She pictured him wingless, beakless, featherless, and speechless—or not changed at all, sitting on Raymunda's dinner plate, battered, cooked, and seasoned to taste.

She stared into the trees, searching for him. As her hope of ever seeing him again started to falter, he came fluttering into view! Her heart leaped with joy as she watched him glide her way. But something wasn't quite right.

"Voltaire! I'm so happy to see you." She jumped down the stairs, and he landed in the palm of her hand. "How do you feel?" she asked, looking at the bird with a good deal of concern.

"I am totally fine, dear Dwana. I mean Wadna. Make that Wanda! Do not be alarmed. My brain at the moment is just a tiny bit scrambled."

"But your feathers—they're green." Wanda couldn't help but stare.

"Oh, that." The bird ruffled his wings. "A lovely hue, the result of mixing chicken yellow with Voltaire blue. Young William has assured me that my natural color will return. One day. Soon."

"Things aren't perfect here, either," Wanda confided. "Wren is not the sister I had hoped for." She told Voltaire all about Wren's constant complaints and how she had tried to take her room. "I don't blame her for being upset," Wanda said. "But I wonder—will she stay bitter forever?" She sighed. "At least you're back to yourself, mostly. And we're all home, and we're safe."

"Well, not exactly," the bird chirped.

"Not exactly? Not exactly to which part?" Wanda asked.

"Let me think," Voltaire leaped from her hand. "I repeated it over and over the entire way here so I wouldn't forget." He started to pace. "Zounds!" He came to a halt. "I've remembered it in record time!" he said, and they both cheered.

"It's the part about being safe." He flew to her shoulder. "You see, when you brought Wren home, you broke the curse on the witches. They can now leave the woods. And I believe one or two, maybe more, might be heading our way. Oh, and one of those witches might be Zane. Yes, definitely Zane. But no worries, dear Danwa. As the great Winston Churchill perhaps once said, 'Success is not final, failure is not fatal: It is the courage to continue that counts.'"

You might think that Wanda would have found all this distressing. She had a spiteful sister. An important book to protect. And now witches to watch out for—more than one, possibly many, and most definitely Zane. But she also had the very best best friend to help her. So Wanda wasn't worried. She wasn't worried one bit.

"If danger arrives on our doorstep, we will try very hard not to run away!" Voltaire proclaimed. "Instead, we will greet it with great confidence! Probably. Most likely."

Wanda agreed.

"What's all the squawking about?" Wren walked out the front door, letting it slam behind her. She squinted at the little green bird perched in Wanda's hand. "Voltaire, is that you?" Her mouth twitched as she fought to remain sour. But she couldn't help it—she laughed.

She sat down on the steps, and Wanda sat beside her—and that's when Wanda noticed the strange, dark pink wand in her hand.

"It's made from the wood of the pink ivory tree," Wren explained. "Raymunda said it was very special, and now I think I know why. It must give an ordinary person powers." The muscles in Wren's face stiffened. "Raymunda used it to trick me. To make me believe I was a witch."

"What kind of spells did you cast?" Wanda tried to hide her excitement. It was clear that Wren was upset talking about Raymunda, and Wanda didn't want to say anything that might anger her, but she really, really wanted to know about that wand. And since her sister seemed pleased by the attention, Wanda continued. "Can you cast spells on a witch with it?"

"I don't know," Wren replied. "I was only allowed to use it for simple things, you know, like warming up hot chocolate, changing the color of my bedspread, and filling the bathtub."

"Do you think it still works?" Wanda asked. "Now that you're . . . here?"

"That's exactly what I was wondering." Wren's lips tightened. "There's one way to find out." She pointed the wand at Voltaire, who was sitting quite comfortably in Wanda's palm.

"Wait!" Before Wanda could shield the bird, a tiny yellow spark flew from the wand's tip. It hit Voltaire, and he let out an odd squeak.

"What did you do to him?" Wanda was furious. She struggled to take a breath. "Voltaire, are you all right?"

"Yes, I am." The bird nodded. "In fact, I'm more than all right. My curiosity has now been satisfied. Thank you, Wren." Voltaire hopped to the ground, and Wanda saw a tiny green egg nestled in the center of her hand. "I must say, it's a very fine feeling to lay an egg."

"And it's a very fine egg!" Wanda laughed, immensely relieved. She gazed sheepishly at Wren. "Sorry I got mad. It's just—"

"Wanda." Voltaire interrupted, pacing in front of both of them. "You have *The*

Book. Wren, you have a magic wand. You two are quite the sorcerers now."

"I guess we are." Wren shrugged and gave a slight smile. Her resolve to resent them seemed to be withering.

"We *definitely* are." Wanda grinned, happy to see Wren's icy mood starting to thaw. "There's no stopping us now!"

With Voltaire and her sister by her side, she knew she could conquer all the creatures from the Scary Wood and any witch who might come their way. Her heart soared with hope, trust, and courage, the best magic of all.

"Let's go inside," she said, rising to her feet, "and see what we can do about hatching this egg."

Save the Date

If you're reading this, that means
you're invited to my wedding.
I'm marrying Wanda.
Leave your name on this page and the
pooka will deliver your invitation.
Watch out. It will be attached to a rock.
Don't say I didn't warn you.

The Royal Prince Frog

Voltaire's Acknowledgments

I would like to acknowledge me, the world-famous Voltaire, for my wonderful and witty quotes that you found in this book. I created them back in the 1700s, and I polished them up this month just for you. Here they are again. Take a look:

"Dare to think for yourself."

"Love truth, but pardon error."

"Everything you say should be true, but
not everything true should be said."

Clever, aren't they?

I would also like to acknowledge the great playwright William Shakespeare, who was terribly misquoted by that witch Raymunda. "Fare is fowl, and fowl is fare." You might remember she said that when she turned me into a chicken. How rude that was!

Here, dear reader, is what Shakespeare actually wrote: "Fair is foul, and foul is fair." Quite different, you'd have to agree—and no mention of poultry whatsoever!

And finally, I would like to acknowledge you, dear reader, for sticking with me and Wanda to this very last moment. And I will thank you without delay and in person—when we meet at Wanda and Prince Frog's wedding. See you there. . . .

Author's Acknowledgments

Thank you, Disney Hyperion and Little, Brown Books for Young Readers, for bringing *Wanda Seasongood and the Almost Perfect Lie* into the world!

Special thanks to Tyler Nevins for his joyful design, and boundless appreciation to editor Stephanie Lurie.

To the incredible Jenn Harney, admiration and cheers for capturing Wanda and the creatures of the Scary Wood with such great humor and flair.

Much gratitude to Megan Tingley, Alvina Ling, Nikki Garcia, Alex Kelleher-Nagorski, and all the wonderful people at Little, Brown who worked on this book.

And, finally, much love to family and friends who joined me on this awesome adventure.